P9-ELD-888

Miklowitz, Gloria D. Anything to Win. July
1989. 160p. Delacorte, $14.95 (0-385-29750-5).
Galley. CH

Steriods—Fiction ‖ Drug abuse—Fiction ‖ Football—Fiction
[OCLC] 88-30909

This simple cautionary tale dramatizes the
danger of steroids in high school athletics. Football captain Cam Potter has a chance at a big
college scholarship—if he puts on 30 pounds
fast. His corrupt coach steers Cam to a supplier.
Impelled by his need for stardom, his belief in his
own immortality, and his father's driving expec-
tations, Cam ignores the health warnings and
ethical issues and swallows dozens of male hormone pills each day. His brother tries to stop
Cam, and the girl he loves rejects him for his
increasingly macho behavior. Finally, as he be-
comes scared about both his aggression and his
sexual impotence, he's also shocked by the terminal cancer of a long-time user and throws the
drugs away. Miklowitz is not as smooth as usual;
there's lots of pop therapy from the brother and
girlfriend (grouchy Dad "can't like himself if you
don't like him") and little complexity of charac-
ter or story. But the issue has been carefully
researched, and jocks and sports fans will be
fascinated by the medical information, the com-
petitive football scene, and the ethical conflict.
Gr. 7–12. —Hazel Rochman *BKL 7/89*

ANYTHING TO WIN

DISCARDED

Also by Gloria D. Miklowitz

THE EMERSON HIGH VIGILANTES

GOOD-BYE TOMORROW

SECRETS NOT MEANT TO BE KEPT

LOVE STORY, TAKE THREE

THE WAR BETWEEN THE CLASSES

THE DAY THE SENIOR CLASS GOT MARRIED

CLOSE TO THE EDGE

THE LOVE BOMBERS

DID YOU HEAR WHAT HAPPENED TO ANDREA?

$ 15.00

ANYTHING TO WIN

Gloria D. Miklowitz

Widefield High School
LIBRARY MEDIA CENTER
Security CO 80911

FIC
MIK
a
'90
BC 36404

Delacorte Press

I am grateful to Nik Larez,
football coach at La Cañada High School,
for his help in explaining football plays
and player mentality,
and for his perceptive comments
on this book.

Published by
Delacorte Press
Bantam Doubleday Dell Publishing Group, Inc.
666 Fifth Avenue
New York, New York 10103

Copyright © 1989 by Gloria D. Miklowitz

All rights reserved. No part of this book may be reproduced or
transmitted in any form or by any means, electronic or
mechanical, including photocopying, recording or by any
information storage and retrieval system, without the written
permission of the Publisher, except where permitted by law.

The trademark Delacorte Press ® is registered in the U.S.
Patent and Trademark Office.

Library of Congress Cataloging in Publication Data

Miklowitz, Gloria D.
Anything to win.

Summary: To increase his chances of winning a college
scholarship, a talented high school quarterback risks
his health by taking anabolic steroids to gain weight.
[1. Steroids—Fiction. 2. Drug abuse—Fiction.
3. Football—Fiction] I.Title.
PZ7.M593An 1989   [Fic]   88-30909
ISBN 0-385-29750-5

Manufactured in the United States of America

July 1989

10 9 8 7 6 5 4 3 2 1

BG

1

Two weeks before the Senior Switch Dance four girls—
four!—all popular and good-looking, asked me to be
their dates. I should have felt great. The guys on the
team teased me about it. My brother, Peter, asked me
what I had that he didn't.

But the truth was, it didn't mean a thing. I didn't
want to go with any of them. The truth was, the one girl
I wished would ask—Laurel Greene—hardly knew I
was alive.

It was no accident that I stood only two bodies away
from Laurel in the lunch line (I always "happened" to
be somewhere near her) when Penny Dravinski made
it five.

"How's it going, Cam?" she greeted, sidling up to me,
right within sight and earshot of Laurel. She put a hand
on my arm as if we were long-time close and said, "If
you're not already spoken for, how about we go to the
switch dance together?"

Penny's a little thing. There's maybe a foot between
the top of her head and my eyes. Glancing sideways to
see if Laurel was watching I smiled down at her raised

face and said, "Thanks, Penny. I'm flattered; mind if I let you know?"

Behind me Kevin, my best friend, stifled a chuckle. I stepped hard on his foot, but as soon as Penny left he poked his head around the kid in front of us and said, "Wanna make it an even half dozen, Laurel?"

"Half dozen what?" she asked, turning around.

"Kevin!" I warned as my face began to burn.

Kevin laughed and danced out of reach. "Six is a lucky number. Cam's just got his fifth invitation to the switch. Wanna make it six?"

Laurel's smile brushed over me and my hands began to sweat. At that moment I could understand why guys said "You can't get near her with a ten foot pole." She ran two fingers behind her ears, sweeping the straight brown hair back from her dark, beautiful eyes. "Why? Now, why would I want to do that?" she asked, as if genuinely curious.

"Kevin!" I warned again.

He ignored me. "You have to ask?"

I could have murdered him, but I had to play it cool. Other kids in line were having a good time eavesdropping, getting a kick out of my discomfort.

"Give me three good reasons why I should ask *him* to be *my* date!" Laurel's lips curled into that enigmatic smile that drove me wild.

I stepped behind Kevin and jammed a hand over his mouth. "One, he's a hunk," he gurgled through my fingers. "Two, he's a good guy. Three, he's captain of the football team."

"Oh?" Laurel said, as if this was all news, as if she never read the sports page in the school paper or never noticed me in whatever classes we had in common, and never saw me with friends.

"So long, guys," I said, stomping out of line and vowing to fix Kevin, first chance. "You can talk about me behind my back now."

"So?" Kevin asked.

"I don't think so," I heard Laurel say as I strode away. "I don't go for jocks."

"Screw you, Kevin Mayer," I said to myself. "And screw you, too, Laurel Greene. I wouldn't date you now if you were the last girl on earth." Fuming, I took my place at the end of the food line. Two minutes later Kevin ambled up, hands in pockets, a silly grin on his freckled face.

So maybe I am a jock. So what? Half the guys at school wish they could be. Why not? If you're good, nobody pushes you for grades. You get respect from everybody, even the teachers. You're having fun doing what you like doing best and girls go crazy just to wear your varsity jacket. The crowds yell your name as if you were a rock star. You get invited to all the parties that count.

Who wouldn't like that?

Laurel is who.

But why? Was it just me, or what?

All the next week those last words of hers buzzed in my head like a swarm of bees and man, did they sting! I didn't know what I'd liked about her in the first place. She was a stuck-up airhead, I decided. She didn't know the first thing about life. Didn't she realize that the only thing that really mattered was winning? Didn't she realize how important sports were? *Are?*

* * *

It wasn't until Friday of the next week that I finally figured the way to make Laurel sit up and take notice and maybe even eat those words.

We were in the locker room, just before practice. It was the usual chaos. Locker doors slamming. Voices echoing. The smell of sweat, dirty socks, and chlorine. Guys swatting towels at each other. You know, the usual.

Kevin had disappeared to smoke a joint. It's become a habit. Used to be he'd take it only before games. Said he got so hyper he needed something to slow him down. I don't judge, he's old enough to know what he can handle. Pot's not for me. I tried it a couple of times but it burns the throat and turns my brain to cotton candy. You got to think fast when you're playing football. You know. You get the ball and you've got a split second to decide who to throw it to, where the guy will be two seconds later, so you can figure at what angle and speed to throw. So pot's not my bag.

But anyway.

Kevin comes back, all smiles, his eyes a little glassy. "Something's going on," he says. "Cooney's yakking with these strangers. Look like scouts to me."

"No kidding!" Unexpectedly, a spurt of adrenaline shot through me. Some time during senior year the college recruiters make the rounds, checking out the high school sports talent for their schools. There are scholarships out there if you're any good. For some guys it's the only way to get to college. Me, for instance.

Until recently I hadn't given a lot of thought to what I'd do when I graduated. Go into the same thing as

Peter, I supposed, my dad's business, laying sprinkler systems. For that you don't need college. So why the sudden excitement?

I didn't know. All I knew was that at that moment the only thing that mattered was going out on the field and showing my stuff. I felt like my feet had wings, like my hands could throw a bullet pass from fifty yards, like a printout of every play I'd ever learned was feeding through my head.

"Okay, guys. Let's get out there and show these guys," I called, grabbing my helmet. "Last one out buys beer for everyone Saturday night."

Two weeks later Coach Cooney asked me to stay after practice. He had something to talk to me about— which wasn't unusual, because he often wanted to go over plays or discuss how he could get more from a particular player. I told Kevin I'd see him later and, after showering, headed for coach's office.

Cooney's a small, skinny guy, with glasses. He looks more like a math teacher, which he is, than a football coach, which he also is. Even though you'd think a little wind could blow him over, the guys respect and like him. Despite his size he's tough and demanding and he won't take any crap, which is why we've been league champs three years running.

"Sit down, Potter," Cooney said, waving at the chair near his desk. "Be with you in a minute." He pushed his glasses up his nose and bent over the play diagrams he was working out. I gazed around the windowless room for the hundredth time in the hundred or so times I'd been there and thought again how much I'd hate being cooped up in a stuffy little hole like this so many hours of my day.

Cooney clipped his pages together and put them aside. Then he straightened out a pile of exam papers, graded, rumor had it, by a guy on the math team.

"Teaching's a pleasure, but grading papers is the pits," he said, removing his glasses and rubbing his eyes with both fists.

"How'd I do?" I reached over to find my paper in the pile of exams but he beat me to it, slamming his hand down on them.

"You did okay. If you put a little more time into studying, you'd be better than average."

"Ah, you know how it is, coach."

"Yeah, I know. You go to school to play football and have a good time. Yeah. I know."

I grinned sheepishly and looked away. What had he called me in to talk about, anyway?

"What's Kevin on?" he asked, unexpectedly.

"Kevin?"

"Yeah, Kevin."

"What do you mean?"

"You know exactly what I mean. I know you guys booze it up on weekends—and maybe even during the week—even though it's against team rules. I suspect some of you have tried coke . . . and I don't approve. But I understand. When you're facing a guy fifty pounds heavier than you and you know he's going to be on top of you and you're going to get hurt, it's a lot easier to hang in there if you're on coke. I understand. But I want it on the record that I don't approve."

"Yeah," I said, staring him straight in the eyes. So

. . . he knew a lot more than we gave him credit for! And he let it go on. Saying he didn't approve cleared him of responsibility, made it okay in his book. Wow. I guess what it came down to was winning. Winning meant everything. Cooney liked being coach of a winning team. He was something of a celebrity. Maybe he even got paid more because of it.

Wow.

"What's he on?" Cooney asked again. He twirled a red pencil around with two fingers on his right hand so its point drilled into the middle finger of his left. "Is Kevin a pothead?"

"How would I know?"

"Don't try to snow me, Potter. You're team captain. You should know. He's your best friend."

I lowered my head and studied my hands.

"You know as well as I do. His reactions are slow. He's too laid-back to get tough."

I didn't answer.

"All right. Now this is what I'm gonna do. I'm telling you now that unless he shapes up, he's off the team."

"Why don't you tell him yourself?" I asked.

He didn't answer right away; my eyes kept going to the hole he seemed to be drilling in his finger.

"I want you to talk to him. It's a warning. I'll be watching."

I shrugged and stood up. I had about as much chance of influencing Kevin as an ice cube has in hell. "Is that what you wanted to talk about?"

Cooney stood also. He dropped the pencil and gathered up the papers on his desk to put into a beat-up plastic attaché case. "Walk me to my car. There's one more thing."

I stood by while he checked his papers, straightened his desk, and grabbed his jacket. The true perfectionist, he looked back before turning off the light and locking the door. Finally we crossed the big, empty gym, the only sound being the occasional squeak of my sneakers on the slick floor. He didn't tell me what was on his mind until we were out of the building in the fading afternoon light.

"You want to go to college, don't you?"

"I don't know. Yeah, sure, I guess so."

"Well, you better make up your mind fast because State's gonna offer you a scholarship."

"Yeah?" I felt a grin start in my chest and spread all through me. Until that moment I hadn't realized that I did care, that I did want to go to college.

"Yeah."

"How come?" I wanted to hear him say it . . . that I was good, better than everyone. But when it came to compliments, Cooney was a miser. "Not bad" in his language translated to "fantastic" in anyone else's.

He glanced my way as if he could read my mind and snorted.

"Come on, coach. They must have said *something*! Why me?"

"They need a good quarterback."

That was about as far as he'd go.

"There's a condition, though."

By now we'd reached his beat-up blue Dodge. It was a joke around school that the oldest cars belonged to the teachers. He unlocked the door and cranked down the window, then he turned back to me. "You're gonna have to put on thirty pounds by January. Thirty pounds. College football's tough, not like what we do here. The players are for real; at your weight and with your build, first game you played they'd break you in two. You willing?"

"Thirty pounds!" I whistled. My mom kids me all the time about the amount of food I put away. Dad says half the food budget goes to what I eat.

"At least. You need the bulk and power if you're to be worth it to them."

"Ye Gads. *Thirty* pounds! That's a lot!"

Cooney nodded, watching my face for an answer. "A full four-year scholarship, remember. Room, board, *and* tuition."

"*How?* I mean, how can I put on that kind of weight? Milk shakes and ice cream sundaes? I already pig out on that kind of stuff and it doesn't put on an ounce."

"There are ways."

"Like?"

"You don't think these big professional athletes get to be the hunks they are by eating Wheaties, do you?"

"They don't?" I pretended innocence. And then I suddenly got what he meant. "You mean—steroids?"

For a long moment we faced each other and a lot was spoken between us that didn't come out in words. "I didn't say that. You did," he finally added.

"You're talking out of both sides of your mouth, Cooney," I felt like saying but bit my tongue instead.

"Interested?" He climbed in the car and slammed the door.

"Sure. Who wouldn't be. Man!"

"Good." He pulled a wallet from his hip pocket and drew a card from it which he handed out the window to me. "Check these guys out. They're very good. They'll have you looking like Charles Atlas in two months."

The card gave an address and phone number and read, "Crescent Body Building Studio. Put weight on? Take it off? We're specialists. Ask for Mike."

"Congratulations, Cam," Cooney said warmly. "You're making the right decision. You won't be sorry. There's not a guy on the team who wouldn't wish he could be in your shoes."

"Yeah," I said, fingering the card. "Thanks."

"See you tomorrow." Cooney started the wheezy engine and pulled away in a cloud of dirty smoke.

And that's when I thought, "So Laurel Greene doesn't like jocks, huh? Just wait till she hears about State! That'll change her tune!"

2

"No kidding?" Pete exclaimed when he heard the news at dinner that night. "Hey, kid! That's great!"

"How come *you* didn't get an offer like that when *you* were in high school?" Dad asked, pointing his coffee cup in Pete's direction.

Pete forced a weak grin. "Not good enough. Isn't that what you want to hear?" He turned to me. "Think he'll ever let me off the hook for not snagging that scholarship they gave O'Neill?"

"You *could* have had it, you know!" Dad went on. "You just didn't have the guts. You got to *want* to win so much that you'll do anything! You just didn't care enough. You could have . . ."

"Come on, Dad. Confess. Aren't you glad? If I'd gone to college, who'd be working his butt off running errands for you all day? Who'd you criticize for not bidding a job high enough, huh?"

"Hey you two; quit it!" I pleaded. "Come on!"

It was so hard to listen to them lately, constantly bickering. Mealtimes were battlefields, with Dad lobbing accusations at Pete and Pete firing back with pain-filled jokes. I loved them both and it hurt to hear them go at each other. Worse, a lot of the arguments seemed to start because Dad used me as the example for Pete to live up to.

Maybe working with Dad wasn't such a great idea for Pete, though it had seemed so when he graduated from high school two years ago. He'd already been working part-time for Dad, just as I am now, and it had been okay. He went out with the work crews, and he dug trenches and cut pipe like he was told, and he made pretty good money. But now that he was on full time and working beside Dad in the office, it was different. Is that how it would be if I went on full time?

"Cam's right, Bill," Mom said, trying to smooth things over. "This is about him, not Pete. Pass me your plate, Cam. If you've got to put on so much weight, you'll have to eat more."

"Honestly, Mom. I can't. If I swallow one more bite I'll burst," I said, clutching my stomach in mock pain.

"Give it here," Pete said, holding his plate out. He knew it would annoy Dad because Dad was always warning him to watch his weight. "Lardball," Dad would sometimes call him. I was tall like my father and lean, with his fair complexion and rust-red hair, but Pete looked like Mom, and was built like her, too—short and compact with a tendency to overweight.

"Cooney said I should join a bodybuilding club," I said, before Dad could pick up on Pete. "What do you think, pops?"

"Sounds like a good idea," he said, smiling warmly. "They'll probably put you on a special diet and design a workout program for you that will do the trick."

"Hey, Pete? What do *you* think?"

"It's up to you, kid," my brother said, with his mouth full of food. "You look okay to me the way you are. But thirty pounds! You sure you want to look like Schwarzenegger?"

"He can handle it. Cam's got a big frame," Dad said. "I could put on twenty pounds and you'd hardly notice."

"But, honey. How will you find the time?" Mom asked. "I mean, what with school work and practice and working out and helping Dad . . ."

"Don't worry, Mom. I'll make time." I hadn't asked for spending money since I was fourteen—which is when I started part-time work for Dad, and I didn't want to have to ask for it now. Besides, it didn't seem right, not pulling my weight, just like Pete. So, no matter, I'd find time.

"Never mind," Dad said. "You concentrate on gaining weight so you get that scholarship! How could we ever come up with that kind of money? No, Cam. I can always hire some young stud to dig ditches. What I can't hire so fast is a guy with the smarts. You get that scholarship. At least one of my sons . . ." He stopped himself at a warning look from Mom.

I concentrated on drawing patterns with my fork in the leftover gravy on the plate, wondering how Pete felt, and wondering, too, what Dad would say if getting that scholarship meant all that I thought it might.

About five o'clock, after school, I drove downtown to the Crescent Body Building Studio. It was on a busy street, next to a stationery store. Just beyond the receptionist I could see a floor of workout equipment—exer-

cise bikes, weight-lifting machines, rowing machines—
a lot of stuff like we have at school. The walls were
mirrored, and most of the equipment was in use. Good-
looking chicks in shorts and T-shirts pumped away on
the bikes. Guys with bulging muscles and wet with
sweat lifted weights, concentration etched in every
crease of their faces.

Two guys wearing green shorts and white polo shirts
with the logo of the studio on front moved around with
clipboards. They'd stop beside someone, maybe adjust
a weight or say something, then move on.

"Can I help you?" the receptionist asked when I
stopped at the switchboard near the entrance. A pretty
blonde, in her early twenties, she put a hand over the
telephone mouthpiece and smiled. I got the impression
that maybe she was talking with a boyfriend.

"I'm here to see Mike," I said, taking a brochure from
the counter. "Name's Potter. Cam Potter. I have an
appointment."

She pressed a button and spoke into a microphone.
"Mike. You're wanted at the front desk." And then,
turning her back to me, she picked up the phone again.

In a little while a guy in his late twenties, with a fifties
haircut, appeared from the back. I watched him cross
the floor, a friendly smile on his face to everyone. He
was of average height, but his shoulder and arm muscles strained the seams of his shirt and his neck had the
girth of a telephone pole. "Cam?" he asked, extending a
hand. "Good to meet you. Mike Taft; call me Mike.
Cooney phoned. Let's go back to my office and talk."

I followed him to a second room, where maybe a half
dozen guys were working out on some of the very good

equipment. No one looked up. Just as in any workout gym everyone seemed totally absorbed in whatever he was doing. In fact, I saw two guys from the team—one on the bench press, sweat drenching his face, and the other lifting dumbbells, eyes on his image in the mirror. Neither returned my greeting.

Mike led me through a locker room, past the showers to a glassed office off to one side, slid the door open, and motioned for me to sit down. It was a small room with shelves along one wall, a file, a message board full of scraps of paper, a cheap wood desk, and a couple of chairs. I took the seat in front of the desk and folded my hands like a kid in church. Crazy as it sounds, I felt uneasy, as if I was about to turn my life over to someone else. My brother's words—did I want to look like a physical freak, like Schwarzenegger—crossed my mind.

"So, Cam . . . I hear you've got a good chance at a four-year scholarship. Cooney says you've got a strong arm, good judgment, accuracy. You're willing to work hard. You're consistent. Ambitious. You're steady."

"Hey! Cooney said that?" I grinned.

"Cooney said that. And more." Mike leaned toward me, across the desk, and I noticed that he had bad acne, like a teenager. "The guys at State are pretty hot for you but they want more power. You'd be competing with bigger guys, guys who weigh maybe forty to eighty pounds more than you. You build muscle, put on twenty to thirty pounds, and there'll be an army of scouts knocking down your door to sign you. Not just State. You'll get all kinds of offers—cars, jobs you get paid for that you don't even have to show up for, girls. You name it."

"Hey hey!" I said, raising my eyebrows.

"All right. Then if that's what you want, I can help."

"Yeah? How long will it take?"

"Two, maybe three months at most."

"What do I have to do?" I nodded behind me. "Work out every day, like those guys out there?"

"Three times a week, thirty to forty-five minutes each time, will do it."

"That's it?"

"That, diet, and some—vitamin pills."

I watched Mike's eyes. They didn't flinch from my face. "Vitamins? What kind?"

Instead of answering my question directly he asked, "Ever been hurt in play? Sure. You don't play football without getting hurt. A million kids play the game in high school, and there are a million injuries a year. So? What'd you do when you got hurt?"

I thought of the times I'd pulled a ligament or twisted my knee, or hurt a shoulder. Cooney sent me to Carbonetti, the team doc, a sports medicine specialist. "Sure I've been hurt. Carbonetti shot me with Xylocaine or cortisone, and I took codeine so I could play and it wouldn't hurt."

"Then you know what it takes. You get hurt playing, you stay in the game. If the pain gets too bad, Carbonetti shoots you with Novocain. You're young. You're strong. You heal fast. Nothing can hurt you for long."

He sounded like Cooney. "I want winners on this team," he says. "I see nothing outstanding about finishing anything but first. You don't want to be the best? Then you don't belong on this team." Along with that lecture came the understanding that nice guys finish last. You win at any cost, within the rules if you can, outside them if you have to. I never questioned his philosophy because it worked. We won. And that's what mattered.

"I know what it takes," I said. "Now, what about these—vitamins?"

He took a key from a ring attached to his belt and unlocked a drawer in the desk. I couldn't see from where I sat but got the impression that it was a deep drawer because he spent a few minutes sorting through whatever was in it and pulled out several small bottles. He placed them on the desk.

"You got a drugstore in there?" I nodded toward the drawer. My hands began to sweat.

He ignored my attempt at humor and instead opened one of the small bottles and dropped a few pills into one hand. "These *are* vitamins. Megavitamins. You'll take three a day from now on." He poured the pills back and handed the bottle to me. "And these . . ." He watched my face as he opened his hand to show me the vial. "These are dianabol. Anabolic steroids. In case you don't know, anabolic means bodybuilding and steroids describe their chemical nature. They're a synthetic— imitation—of the male hormone testosterone."

I took a deep breath and must have shrunk back in my seat because Mike said, "They won't hurt you, you know. A lot of athletes use them. They increase muscle mass and body weight, just what you need. You take this, work out the way I tell you, eat the foods I say— and I guarantee in six weeks you'll be the guy State wants."

"Do I have to? Isn't it illegal?" I asked, hearing my voice crack.

Mike waved at someone behind me and his eyes lost their warmth. He closed a hand around the vial and withdrew it. "Maybe Cooney was wrong about you. You a wimp? Maybe that scholarship isn't so important to you."

"No! No! Wait!" I said. "I just have some questions! Sure I want the scholarship!"

He studied me across the desk for a long moment, as if he couldn't quite decide if he could trust me. Then he said, "We're not talking about legality. A lot of professionals use it. College athletes are using it. You need that winning edge. You're competing with guys as good as you, with more power, so you do what you have to to win. That's the bottom line."

I fidgeted in my seat, hooked my legs around the chair, ran my fingers over the torn plastic of the seat cushion. What about good sportsmanship and fair play? Didn't that count at all? But I didn't ask that. Instead I said, "What about side effects? You may as well give me the whole story."

"I wouldn't worry about that at all, Cam," Mike said. "I've been on steroids for years, and it hasn't hurt me a bit. Look at me." He flexed his biceps. Fantastic. "I feel great. I look great. You know those two guys on your team who were working out in the other room? How do you think they got to look that way?"

"Bud? Warren?"

"The same."

"But . . . but . . . I read about side effects, it seems

to me. Liver cancer, sterility . . . impotence. I mean
. . . impotence! What about it?"

He laughed and stood up. "I wouldn't worry about
that at all, kid. You're a horny male and you'll stay that
way. Now I gotta get back inside. What do you say?" He
held the two vials out to me. "Want to start today?"

I stood also, but my head was whirling. It was one
thing to talk about using steroids, and another to actually take them. Still, I held out my hand to receive the
pills.

"Good," Mike said, sliding open the glass doors.
"Now put those away and follow me. I'll show you your
locker, explain your diet, get you started on your
workout program. Believe me, Potter. You won't be
sorry. You'll be a hero. You'll be the envy of all the guys
on the team when you get those offers. And the girls
. . . well. I guarantee, they'll be knocking down your
door to get at you!"

3

"How can you be so cruel, Cam! Put an end to their misery!" Kevin teased. We were showering after practice, and he'd been riding me for days about which girl I'd go with to the switch dance. "Don't you see them watching you around school, practically holding their breaths?" he shouted above the noise of the water. "They're probably sitting on their phones, afraid they'll miss your call! Man!"

"Knock it off, Kev," I shouted back. "I'm going with Amy Wilson. Satisfied?" I turned my face up to the showerhead, opened my mouth, closed my eyes, and let the hot water pelt my skin.

"Well, hallelujah!" Kevin cried so everyone around could hear. "He made up his mind! We can have his leftovers! There'll be four disappointed females scurrying around, looking for last-minute dates!"

I turned off the water and grabbed my towel, flicking it at Kevin's ass so he hopped away as if mortally wounded. Kevin's image of my popularity was flattering, but I had no illusions about why I'd been asked to the switch. Girls like to be paired with the captain of the football team. Most girls, I should say. Obviously, not Laurel. And it didn't matter much if the guy had a nothing personality and beans for brains.

Kevin and I left the locker room together to go to the parking lot. We usually spent the half hour or so before each of us had to go to our jobs—Kevin delivered Domino pizzas—yakking about this or that at the nearest fast-food hangout. This time we met at McDonald's and took a booth in the back with our milk shakes and his fries and onion rings.

"What's with Cooney?" Kevin asked, running a hand through his shoulder-length hair. "He's been on my case all week!"

I took a long, refreshing swig of the chocolate shake, figuring I was consuming at least 600 of the 4300 calories Mike said I had to get each day. I wiped my mouth with the back of my hand and decided this was the time to level with him about Cooney's warning.

"Christ!" Kevin exclaimed, when he heard the ultimatum. He jabbed a fry into a mound of ketchup. "What's he down on me for? He's got you on steroids! And what about Reese? He's gotta know he's on coke!"

"Reese? Tom Reese, our linebacker?"

"Where ya been, Cam? Got your head on backwards?"

"How would I know? Reese and I aren't exactly buddies, you know," I said, sarcastically, but of course I should have known. Reese could be an enraged bull on the field and high as a kite after a game, then he'd suddenly fall apart. I began to review the other team members and wondered who else might be on coke or amphetamines. Man. How dumb could I be?

Kevin shoved the plate of onion rings across the table almost as a peace offering, but I shook my head. Fried food was a no-no on the new high-protein, high-carbo-hydrate diet.

"Okay, so you didn't know. But you must have sus-pected," he said.

"Yeah." I took another gulp of milk shake. "I should have."

"So, why's Cooney so pissed? All I'm doing is a little pot. Would he be happier if it was coke?"

"You really think Cooney knows about Reese?" I asked.

"Come on, Cam." He stared at me for a long minute. "Cooney's for Cooney, that's all. He pushes his players so they'll get scholarship offers. Just think what it does for his image. Think how he must feel when he tells the new freshmen, 'Work your butts off and you, too, can win scholarships like the guys last year!' "

"Then to hell with this steroid stuff," I said. "I can build muscle and add weight without this." I pulled the pill bottle out of my jacket pocket and dumped the pills in the empty milk shake carton. "Let's go. I'm due at my workout." I stood up, crumpled the milk carton, and dropped it in the wastebasket on the way to the door.

"As for Cooney's ultimatum," Kevin announced, trot-ting along beside me and licking his fingers, "you can tell him he can stuff it. The day he tells me how to live my life is the day I say good-bye. Football's not that important."

* * *

Amy looked terrific when I picked her up for the dance. She wore this long blue thing with a kind of scarf around the butt which tied in front. It made her look tall, which she was anyway, and graceful, and brought out the blue of her eyes. She almost made me forget that the main reason I'd accepted her invitation was totally selfish: I hoped Laurel would be there, and if she was, I wondered what kind of guy she'd have asked. And whether I'd get a chance to dance with her.

"Oh, Cam," Amy cooed when I handed her an orchid corsage. "How sweet of you! How thoughtful! You pin it on."

It didn't seem especially thoughtful considering she was paying the tab for the dance. And she'd told me twice what color dress she'd be wearing. But still, it made me feel good. Amy's like that. She always finds something nice to say to people. Which probably accounts for her popularity.

It wasn't hard making conversation with her either, because we knew lots of guys in common and saw a lot of each other. I'd pass her in the quad right after school when I was heading for football practice. As head cheerleader maybe she'd be leading the girls in some new cheer. Or I'd see her with the others spread all over the lunch tables painting big paper banners to hang around the school. And she always had a smile for me.

So why did I prefer Laurel?

"Felice is saving a place at her table," Amy said as we checked in at the dance. Warren's there with Penny, and Kevin's there with Cheryl."

"Warren with Penny? Penny Dravinski?" I tried to hide my amusement.

"Sure. Why?" Amy squeezed my arm. "Oh, you silly. So what if he's twice her height? She likes tall guys. So do I."

"And I like tall girls," I said, taking her arm and walking into the gym. "Say! The place looks great. The decorating committee did a *terrific* job."

The big, cold room was softened by the crowd of kids, all in their best clothes, and by the colorful decorations. Lots of bright crepe paper spanned the walls and helium balloons dangled from the ceiling. Even the basketball hoop was decorated so it resembled a big pot of flowers. Tables, covered with paper cloths and surrounded with chairs, lined the sides of the room, leaving the center open for dancing.

Amy took my hand and led the way through the crowd toward the table her friends had reserved, when the music began. Instantly the floor filled up with dancers. The strong beat went straight to the nervous system. I swung Amy around and, grinning, let myself go.

It wasn't until later in the evening, while the group of us sat at the table horsing around, nibbling pretzels, and sipping soft drinks, that I saw Laurel.

Amy was telling us about this Eddie Murphy video she'd rented and we were all laughing as she described some of the scenes. Suddenly I caught sight of Laurel, dancing by in a white dress, her large, dark eyes looking my way. Who can account for physical attraction? I don't think she really saw me, but that one quick glimpse of her had the same effect as when I've just run a red light and there's a police car nearby.

"Hey, Cam?" Amy queried, nudging me back to attention. "Did you hear that? Wasn't that funny?"

I smiled reassuringly and tried to get interested in the conversation again, but my eyes kept sweeping the dance floor in hopes Laurel would look my way.

Kevin disappeared, presumably to bring back more drinks, but I figured he made a pit stop to smoke a couple of joints. "I'm not like you, Cam," he told me once. "Girls scare me. This is the only way I can relax."

"Yeah," I'd said. "I understand." But I didn't, quite.

Kevin started drinking when he was ten, and by the time I met him he was drunk most of the school day. I don't know how come the teachers didn't pick up on it; he'd go to class after lunch and fall asleep. But one day he quit, just like that! He said he suddenly realized that he didn't want to be like his father and grandfather, who were both alcoholics.

I really admired him for that. But then he started smoking pot. As far as I could see, Kevin was as addicted to pot as he'd ever been to alcohol. When I told him that, taking a big chance that he'd never talk to me again, he said, "You don't know the first thing about it. Pot's not addictive."

Maybe. For him, it sure seemed to be.

Anyway. Kevin disappeared, Cheryl and Amy went off to the powder room, and the others were out on the dance floor, leaving me by myself. I decided to mosey around and say hello to a few friends. Hoping, of course, to run into a pretty dark-haired girl in a white dress, named you-know-what.

"Well, hello!" I said, beginning to sweat as soon as I spotted her in a group of kids I knew. The guy she was

with wore glasses and could have been on the basketball team, he was so tall. He stood, one hand on her
back, as if he owned her.

She turned around and for an instant didn't seem to
recognize me, but then that mocking smile took over.

"Care to dance with . . . a jock?" I smiled. Maybe I
was out of line, but for a second there I thought she
blushed.

"Well . . ." She hesitated, glanced at her date. But
the guy was really going on about the CIA and central
America or something. "Sure. Why not." She slipped
out of the circle, murmured something about being
back in a few minutes, and followed me.

I took her hand, wiping my palms first so I wouldn't
give away my excitement, and led her to the dance
floor.

They were playing a new Madonna album—loud and
fast. We faced each other, eyes locked, not talking, not
even touching. She did her thing and I did mine. But
man, talk about turn-ons!

When the number ended, she said, "Thanks. You're a
good dancer. *For a jock.*" That smile again.

I chuckled. "Do you always stick a knife in a compli-
ment?"

Even in the dim light I could tell she blushed.

I held out my arms as a slow piece began, afraid she'd
walk off, having done her duty. But she surprised me.
She checked her date, who was still talking a blue
streak, shrugged, and moved as smooth as satin into my
arms.

The shock of her body against mine removed all
power of thought and speech for the length of the

dance. Not until the music ended and she pulled away did I realize what a dud I must seem. Obviously, she liked guys who had opinions, and expressed them, like the guy she'd invited. And here I'd spent the last three minutes, the only three I'd been granted, the three minutes I should have employed to impress her that I was more than a dumb jock, without speaking a word.

I cleared my throat. "Nice," I said, at a loss for words. "Can I see you again?"

"Again?" She laughed and started back to her date. "There hasn't been a *first* time," she said, smiling at me over her shoulder.

Why did I bother with her! Flustered, I said, "You know what I mean. You going with that guy? I'd like to take you out."

"Oh." She stopped a few feet from her friends and turned to me. "Am I going with him? No. Not him or anyone. But what's the use? You may be a nice guy, but I don't think we have a thing in common."

I felt the blood rise to my face. "Is that so? Well, maybe you're right." From somewhere beyond my twisted tongue came a string of words full of venom, all spoken silently. But just before I walked away I said, "You know what, Laurel? I never have liked snobs."

If Laurel had an answer, I didn't hear it, because within seconds I'd crossed the dance floor swearing to myself that if I ever spoke to Laurel again, I'd need my head examined.

4

"Know how the French fatten their geese before killing them?" Peter asked. A sly grin twisted his lips as we packed the truck with tools and leftover pipe from the sprinkler installation we'd just completed. We'd tested the system for leaks and for spread, and could take off for the next job, leaving the low-paid laborers Dad hired to fill in the trenches.

"How do the French fatten their geese before killing them?" I asked, already getting his drift.

"They force-feed them, stuffing their craws with grain or whatever, whether they're hungry or not." He glanced at me sideways, suppressing a grin.

"That so?"

"I've been watching you these last few days. You remind me of the geese."

I laughed with him. In fact I laughed a lot harder than it was funny because it was sadly true. It's no easy thing downing 4300 calories a day—hungry or not. In the last week I'd been doing what the French did to their geese —force-feeding myself. And without taking the steroids, I'd only put on a pound.

"Wanna drive?" Pete tossed me the keys and went

around to the passenger side of the truck. He plugged a tape into the tape deck and turned the sound way up. Heaven, according to my brother, is driving down the Ventura Freeway in a four-wheel drive, listening to Pink Floyd.

Still, some of our best talks have been with music playing in the background. Maybe that's because you know you don't *have* to say anything then, or maybe because there's not so much going on around you so you can think.

I remember sitting in my brother's room when I first learned about sex. We were listening to Peter, Paul and Mary on an old record player; "Blowin' in the Wind" I think it was. And I remember hearing "Strawberry Hill" when we worried together about Mom and Dad arguing over her wanting to go back to work so we could go to college if we wanted. And Dad shouting that he was the breadwinner and if his kids wanted college it was up to him to find the money.

And now, with Pink Floyd on the stereo, and driving onto the Ventura Freeway, I turned to my brother and asked, "How can you stand working for Dad the way he treats you?"

Peter lit a cigarette and put his feet up on the dashboard. "It won't be forever. I'm trying to save up enough to move into a place of my own. Besides," he added, "I kinda feel sorry for the old man."

"Why?" I glanced around at the slowing traffic, always alert since reading about the freeway snipers, of those in nearby cars. To my right a good-looking blonde smiled at me from a Mercedes convertible driven by a guy twice her age. To the left, and pulling ahead, was a truck packed with blank-faced migrant workers, leaning against each other as if they'd just put in a hard day's work. "How could you feel sorry for Dad?"

"Because he hates himself, which is why he takes it out on me."

"Huh?"

Peter blew smoke rings thoughtfully at the roof of the truck. "Figure it out. You'd think he'd be proud that his oldest son chose to go into business with him. But is he? No. Because down deep he has no respect for what he does. What he wishes *he* could have done—that *I* could have done—was what he hopes *you* can do. Go to college on a *scholarship.* Because he sure can't afford to let you go any other way."

I reached over and turned the music lower, then gripped the steering wheel and concentrated on the road ahead. "Why didn't you try, Pete?"

"Everybody loves a winner," he exclaimed, jamming his half-smoked cigarette into the ashtray.

"But you were a winner! You were as good a receiver as I am a quarterback any day!"

"Not good enough. Don't you know the statistics? A million kids play football in high school. Maybe one in twenty-five of those get to play in college, and not all of them are on scholarships. I just wasn't good enough, that's all. I wasn't willing to 'go the extra mile,' in Dad's words." He checked the clipboard on his lap. "Take the next exit and go north."

For the next few minutes we didn't speak. Peter turned the volume up again as I moved to the off ramp. In a complete change from the sarcasm of a few minutes before, he said, "Anyway, who cares about college?

371. K05 4

I hate being cooped up with books all the time. This is the life. I'm outdoors a lot . . . and except for having to work with Dad, I couldn't be happier."

I thought about Peter and my father as I half tuned out Cooney's pep talk at the next team practice. We were sitting in a classroom, just before going out to the field. Friday we'd be playing San Marino, an important game. Cooney, flanked by the four assistant coaches, paced the floor spouting fire and brimstone. He should have been a preacher. He raised and lowered his voice with dramatic flair, talking about commitment. To ourselves, to the team, to winning—and so forth. I'd heard the same stuff in one form or another often enough before so I could follow Cooney with my eyes while my brain explored its own paths.

What I thought about was love, particularly love of father for son and son for father—and just what it all meant. I wanted to go to college, sure, but a big part of my desire was connected with pleasing Dad. All my life I'd looked to Dad for approval, guided what I did by how he'd react. Was that the way it worked in all families? And should my father love me more because of what I *might* achieve, and Peter less, because he'd failed in some way to fulfill Dad's dream? How complicated love seemed, especially when I guessed that Peter, for all his complaints about pops, probably loved him even more than I did.

So what was it all about, anyway? Shouldn't love come without strings attached? Shouldn't Dad love us, regardless of what we achieved?

Kevin leaned toward me from across the aisle and held a hand to the side of his mouth. "Think Cooney's ever considered becoming a TV evangelist?"

"You got something to say, Mayer?" Cooney asked, alert, as always, to everything going on in the room. He stopped in midstride and crossed his arms over his chest. All heads turned our way. "You're so good out on the field that you don't need to listen? You know something about football that I don't? How about enlightening us?"

The heat rose to my face. Kevin rolled his eyes skyward and slid low in his seat.

Cooney stared Kevin down for another few seconds, then dismissed us to the field. "Potter. Stay a minute."

I stayed in my seat while the guys filed out of the room, helmets tucked under their arms, followed by the assistant coaches. Then I went up to Cooney.

"How's it going?" he asked, checking through papers on a clipboard.

"You mean with Mike?"

He nodded, not looking up.

"Fine. I go down three times a week. He's got me on a program to build stamina and strength. I'm eating like an elephant. Everything's fine."

"Mike tells me you only put on a pound. That's not enough. By this time it should be more like four or five. You taking the—vitamins—he gave you?" This time he looked up.

"Sure I'm taking them," I said, only after a second's hesitation. He'd asked about vitamins, not steroids.

"Well, keep at it. Maybe your system is reacting slowly and you'll catch up. I want to see you get that scholarship, Cam. You'll make us all proud. It means a lot to you, your parents, too, *and* the school. *Don't screw up.*"

I swung my helmet around by its strap, waiting for more. But Cooney had said all he intended. "We've got a lot to do before we meet San Marino Friday. Let's go." He put a hand on my shoulder as if we were close buddies, and together we jogged out to the football field.

I didn't notice Laurel until Kevin pointed her out. She was sitting in the stands, doing homework. Homework? Here? The only girls who did that, or pretended to, were girlfriends, or hoping-to-be girlfriends, of guys on the team.

"Two bucks she's here to watch you," Kevin offered as we bent over in the huddle.

"Fifty-eight sweep. Thirty counter!" I called, ignoring him, but rattled by her presence. "Hike!"

A minute later, with the ball tightly clutched under one arm, I zigzagged over the field looking for an opening from which to throw. Distracted for a mere second by a blurred vision of Laurel watching, I stumbled. That's all it took. A one-second loss of concentration and suddenly there were five guys on top of me, five guys landing on my back, my legs, my shoulders, my head. In the dark tunnel of bodies, before I passed out from the searing pain in my arm, I smelled dust and sweat and heard Cooney's angry whistle.

"Where the hell were you?" Cooney accused when I came to. "Where the hell was your concentration?"

Kevin helped me to my feet while the rest of the team backed away, scared off by Cooney's fury.

"Easy there, Mayer! He may have broken something!" In a more concerned voice he bent over me and asked, "You okay, Potter? Anything hurt?"

I grimaced as I tested my legs. My arm felt like it had been torn from its socket. My neck hurt. My legs felt like I'd just walked through a forest of knives.

"Get him to the injury room," Cooney ordered, taking my arm. "Johnson!" he called to one of the assistant coaches. "Take over!"

Five minutes later, disregarding my protests that I felt fine now, the team doctor went over me, and confirmed I'd live. No broken bones. Just a bad sprain and torn ligament. Nothing a few days of therapy in the whirlpool couldn't fix.

Cooney stood by, arms crossed, concern and irritation showing in his pursed lips.

I tried to forestall the lecture I saw coming. "Come on, coach. Lighten up. I'm gonna be fine. See?" Despite the pain I stood up and grinned, but the color must have left my face because Cooney bellowed, "Sit down! Don't play games with me, Potter. I'd like to know why this happened!

"Ah, you know. Football's a rough game," I said.

"Baloney! The truth is, you weren't paying attention!"

I supported my right arm by holding it at the elbow with my left. It was hurting like the devil. Why didn't he leave me alone instead of putting me through this third degree! "Okay," I admitted. "So my mind wandered for a second. Okay?"

"You play football, your mind doesn't wander!" Cooney spewed back. "You need total concentration! I've told you that a hundred times! Just look what's happened to you! I don't want you getting hurt! You've got a terrific future in sports ahead. Think what the damage would be if you were playing with the big guys —in college! You're not heavy enough! Not strong enough! Why do you think it's so important for you to put on that weight, build those muscles?" He pursed his lips in distaste and pushed his glasses back up his nose.

A funny expression crossed Cooney's face, as if he suddenly realized something he hadn't before. In a soft, almost wheedling tone he said, "You leveling with me? I don't see how come you've hardly put on any weight if you're doing what you're supposed to do. Tell me, Potter. You leveling with me?"

"For God's sake, leave the kid alone, Cooney!" the doctor said, taking a vial of cortisone from his bag and sticking a needle into it. "He's in pain. Can't you see?"

If Cooney thought I'd admit I hadn't taken the dianabol, he had another think coming. But he'd gotten his point across. If I hoped to compete with guys thirty and more pounds heavier than I, and I had a time limit of two months to prove it possible, well . . . maybe Mike and Cooney knew what they were talking about.

"Where's the pain?" the doctor said, standing over me, needle poised. He pressed gently along my arm.

Cooney about-faced and strode out of the room.

Between ice packs and whirlpool baths in the injury room I had plenty of time to think. I thought about the dianabol pills and figured I better ask Mike for more.

And I thought about Laurel. Why had she been sitting in the stadium, watching the football practice? And what did she think when she saw me go down like a clumsy ape under a load of guys?

5

Two days later I found out.

Limping down the hall from chem lab I stopped at a drinking fountain to swallow my midday quota of pills —a salmon-colored megavitamin and the blue dianabol. Every time I passed a mirror in the last two days I found myself checking out my image. Did twenty-four hours of steroid taking make a difference? Was it imagination, or did my shoulders look heavier?

It was between periods and kids pressed by me in the usual rush to get to class on time. I scrunched sideways to avoid the crush of bodies and the chance I'd get bumped. I didn't need any extra stress on the very sore parts just beginning to heal. Straightening up and wiping the water from my mouth with the back of a hand, I found myself looking almost straight into Laurel Greene's eyes. I think my face must have turned the color of a ripe plum and my first instinct was to turn my back and run—well, hobble—in the opposite direction.

"Hi," she said in a tentative, almost shy way.

"Hi," I answered, very much on guard, shifting my books and checking my watch. The vision of Laurel sitting in the stands and watching me go down raced across my mind. "Well, gotta go." I quickened my pace and tried to hide the limp.

"Wait!" She fell in beside me. "Were you hurt badly? It looked like a dozen guys piled on top of you!"

"You were there?" I asked, pretending ignorance. "What's a nice girl like you, who doesn't like jocks, doing at football practice?" Maureen, a friend of Amy's from the cheerleading squad, smiled at me in passing. I swung around, deliberately turning my back on Laurel and called out, "Hey, Maureen! When you see Amy would you tell her I'll be by this afternoon?"

"I wanted to . . . I thought . . . I blamed . . ." Laurel went on as if she didn't notice, then in exasperation, "Oh, never mind!"

"What? You thought you ruined my concentration on the field, that you had anything to do with what happened?" I gave a good imitation of a laugh.

"You know, Cam Potter," she replied with a voice straight out of the freezer, "I should have trusted my instincts. I was right the first time I saw you. I thought maybe I'd been hasty and owed you an apology." She shook her head vigorously. "We really *don't* have anything in common." She turned abruptly and pushed her way through the traffic.

I plodded on to my next class, replaying our conversation. Dumb, I told myself. She was trying to apologize and you blew it. Very dumb.

The hall crowds were thinning. Most of the kids had already disappeared into their classrooms. Just as I reached English the bell rang. Mrs. Taylor is a great one for putting stuff on the board that she expects us to copy straight into our notebooks. She was already in place, scratching away with the chalk. Shoot, I said, turning around and loping back down the hall. It's now or never.

It was no coincidence that I knew precisely where to find Laurel. I'd memorized her schedule, and every chance I had, haunted the halls near her classes in hopes of bumping into her. How's that for being soft in the head?

"Laurel!" I called, my voice echoing in the near-empty hall. "Laurel! Wait up!"

She had just opened the study-room door but stopped, a hand on the knob, the expression on her face not encouraging.

I hobbled closer. "Look. I'm sorry. We started off all wrong. What do you say we start again?" Before she could answer, I stuck out a hand. "I'm Cam Potter and I think you're beautiful and I'd like to get to know you better. What do you think?" I flashed my most charming smile.

She shook her head as if she thought me crazy, but a small smile played at her lips. For an instant she took her hand off the knob and touched my outstretched palm. "Okay, truce. Okay, call me; I'm in the book."

I limped back to English with a big grin on my face. Taylor gave me a dirty look as I slid into my seat. Still smiling, and like the good boy I am, I picked up a pen, opened my notebook, and started copying from the board.

While the team practiced out on the field, I lay in the injury room whirlpool letting the hot, swirling waters do their work—and thinking. I'd dated, even gone with, a dozen girls since high school, and not one of them made me feel the way I did about Laurel. Why? I hardly knew her, yet whenever I got within two feet of her, strange things happened to my body. My mouth went dry, my brain short-circuited, and electric pulses shot through my wrists.

"Maybe it's herpes," is what Kevin said when I first tried to describe it.

"Yeah, sure," I said, ignoring his tease. "But why? She's not as pretty as Amy! She has no interest in sports. She thinks I'm a moron whose only interest is sex."

"She's wrong about that?"

"Big help you are, pal."

So—sitting there in the whirlpool, reviewing all this, I still asked myself what made me like Laurel so much I'd make a fool of myself.

Because—and I hated to admit it—she was the first girl I'd ever met who didn't think I was so great.

Because—there's something exciting about winning the game when all odds are against you.

Because—Laurel had to be pretty sharp to see what other girls didn't, that behind all that macho stuff there wasn't a whole lot of—substance.

Hey, come on, my positive side argued. Don't be so down on yourself. You're a fair student. A better than average quarterback. What are you complaining about?

And? And?

There had to be more to a guy than that, I told myself. What happens ten years down the line if I don't make pro? Because isn't that what it's all about? Becoming a professional, with all that fame and big bucks?

So what have you got then, other than a big box of

clippings about what a great guy you once were—out on the playing field.

Believe me. That kind of thinking makes you humble pretty fast. And that's about the mood I was in when I phoned Laurel that evening to ask her out.

The phone call went like this:

"Laurel?" I felt like fourteen again, and the first time I'd ever called a girl. Even my voice rose in a preadolescent squeak.

"Cam . . ." she answered, and I could just imagine that quiet, secret smile.

I searched my mind frantically for something bright to say and came up blank.

"Ball's in your court, Potter," she said.

Grasping at straws, I asked, "You play tennis?"

"So so."

"Good!" My voice settled down. I hadn't held a tennis racket since I was four, when I used one to sift sand for the fort I was building and then hit Peter over the head because he was trying to take the racket away. "At last we found something in common."

"You play? Are you any good?"

"As a matter of fact, no. Where I grew up, tennis was considered a sissy game. I don't play, but I'd like to learn. I may even be good, who knows? Make a deal with you. Teach me how to play tennis, and I'll teach you how to play football."

She laughed. "I can just see me suited up in one of those things with the big shoulder pads and helmet, with those black stripes on my cheeks. What are they for, anyway?"

"You really want to know? You really want to understand about football and maybe come to a game sometime?"

"Don't rush me," she said. "I'll see. Meanwhile, I am curious why any normal human being with even a minuscule brain would let himself be chased, knocked down, kicked, jumped on, and flattened, all for a stupid ball."

"Watch it there, woman," I said, cradling the receiver and smiling. "You're talking about the sport I love."

"I'd sure like to understand why."

She was the first girl I'd ever met who asked me something like that. All the rest took it for granted that just being on the team qualified me for hero status. "Tell you what, Laurel. I'll pick you up Saturday morning. You bring the rackets and I'll bring the balls." I stopped at the double meaning and covered my mouth so she wouldn't hear me laugh. "And we'll take it from there."

6

Saturday marked the beginning of the second week on steroids, the third on the diet and exercise program. Right after my shower I stepped on the scale as I did each morning, to check my weight. Up seven pounds! Six in the last week alone. Great! I pulled on tennis shorts and went to stand before the closet mirror. Not bad. Legs seemed more muscular, shoulders and arms more massive. I had gained power in my throwing arm; that I knew from practice.

"Hey, *gorgeous*! Admiring yourself?" Peter asked from the doorway.

"Seven pounds! Pretty good, huh?"

"Not bad." He came to stand beside me at the mirror. If it wasn't for a resemblance around the eyes and mouth, we'd never pass for brothers. Though five inches shorter than I, he weighed almost the same. His lips curled in self-disgust and he turned away quickly.

"What's with the cute white shorts?" he asked as I pulled on a polo shirt.

"Gonna play tennis with a girl." Sheepishly I added, "It's Laurel. She said she'd teach me."

He dropped down on my bed, picked up an old

Sports Illustrated from the pile on the floor, and aimlessly flipped through the pages. "You know, Cam. I've been reading about athletes and *steroids*."

"Oh?" A bolt of electricity charged through me as, back to him, I picked up a comb.

"Yeah. That stuff's dangerous." His eyes met mine in the mirror.

"Suppose so. Used in excess." I put down the brush and went to the closet for a jacket.

"You can get cramps, insomnia, heart palpitations, high blood pressure. And that's just for starters."

"No kidding?"

"You on them, Cam?"

"Hey!" I turned abruptly, holding a finger to my lips and pointing to the open door. I strode across the room and shut it, feeling the heat rise to my face. "That's a funny question!"

"Is it?" Pete dropped the magazine on the floor. "You are. I knew it."

"So what? It's no big deal! I won't be taking it forever. All I've gotta do is put on thirty pounds. It's not going to hurt me."

"Hey, Cam, don't. You're still growing. Why do you want to upset your hormone balance with a sudden overload of testosterone?" Pete patted his pockets in the all-too-familiar gesture of looking for cigarettes.

My eyes went instantly to the ashtray I keep just for him. I plucked it off the dresser and jammed it down in front of him. "Look who's talking! You smoke two packs a day. You're poisoning your lungs. What's the matter with you? Got a death wish?"

He calmly pulled a cigarette from his pack, examined

it a second, then put it between his lips. Just as calmly he scratched a match, and stared at me as he lit the cigarette and took a deep drag. Then he deliberately blew the smoke in my direction.

"There's nothing more disgusting than cigarette smoke!" I cried, waving a hand to sweep the smoke away. "I don't know why you're making such a big deal of it. I *want* that scholarship. Don't you want me to get it? Besides, like I said, it's not forever!"

"What's *it*? You seem to be having trouble saying the word. *Steroid*. That's what IT is." Peter cradled the ashtray and rose to his feet. "And if you think you 'won't be taking *it* forever,' think again."

"Think what?" I threw my jacket over one shoulder and stared him down.

"Figure it out," he said. "Once you start, the temptation's always there. There's always someone stronger or bigger than you. When—*if* you get to play college football, the pressures will be even greater. You think you'll quit then?" He stubbed his cigarette into the ashtray and went to the door. "Not to mention the whole big issue of *ethics*. But who am I to talk, right? You're old enough to make up your own mind. Just don't say I didn't warn you."

"What's with you guys?" Mom asked, hands on hips, watching as, glowering at each other, we took seats at the breakfast table. I really was annoyed. Pete had no right talking to me like that. He knew the score as well as I. I'm not the kind of guy who'll get in trouble that way. Some guys take more than they should, or don't eat a balanced diet, or take it for years without stopping. And if it was really dangerous, would Cooney have sent me to Mike? And would Mike be giving it to other guys, and taking it himself?

"So? You guys lose your tongues? Why are you throwing daggers at each other?" Mom asked.

"It's nothing, Mom," Pete said. "Just a little disagreement." He smiled just the way Mom does, head slightly tilted and eyes twinkling. "We were comparing physiques, and Adonis, here, made me a little jealous, that's all."

I threw Pete a grateful glance, but his coverup didn't change a thing. The trouble with him was envy, all right. From as far back as I could remember he wanted to look like me. And maybe he didn't *really* want me to succeed. Why should he? It would only make things tougher for him.

But as I thought about our conversation, what really bugged me had nothing to do with how the steroids could hurt me. It had to do with ethics. With taking a drug without a doctor's prescription, a drug that would give me an advantage over other guys my age competing for that same scholarship.

"Follow through! Follow through! This way!" Laurel called from across the tennis court to me later that morning. Again she went through the motions of what she expected me to do.

She'd been instructing me for almost an hour. The first minutes were spent running after the balls I couldn't hit, but now we were enjoying some nice rallies. She was good—graceful and strong. She probably began playing as a kid, taking lessons from a pro. At the same age, I was up to my ankles in dirt, playing any kind of sandlot ball the kids in our housing project would let me in on.

"Cam Potter! Pay attention!" she cried as my attention wandered to how cute she looked in the short white tennis dress that exposed long, tanned legs, and the way her dark hair escaped from her pink sweatband.

When I didn't quite get the swing she wanted, she groaned and, exasperated, strode down the court to my side and took my arm. "This way. See? Now do it again!"

"Like this?" I asked, deliberately doing it wrong so she'd have to show me again. She smelled faintly of lemon. I could see a bead of sweat at her throat and a line of irritation forming at her brow. I liked her this way, feisty and hard to please.

"You're going to be good once you get the hang of it," she said with genuine satisfaction, as we left the court a little later. She pulled off her sweatband and shook out her thick, dark hair. "You could develop a mean serve. You've got the strength. All you need is accuracy."

"Good. How about doing this again tomorrow?"

She smiled. "How about next week?"

"Great. Now, how about your lessons in football? Next game's Friday. We can go out afterwards."

"Thanks, but I don't think I can."

"Why not?" I asked, surprised and disappointed.

"I think I'll be in Palm Springs."

"Oh?" When she didn't elaborate I began to worry who she might be going with. Her family? A boyfriend? Palm Springs isn't a high school hangout, except during holidays like Christmas and Easter when the resort is taken over by guys our age for partying. So how come Laurel was going there?

"Well, then," I said, trying to prolong our date. "How about a drink or something, right now? Orange juice? A milk shake?" We had reached the car and I opened the door for her. "You'd be doing me a favor. I have to pump another six hundred calories into me before lunch."

She tossed the rackets in the back seat and turned to me, incredulous. "What?"

I explained about the scholarship possibilities and the special diet to gain weight and how I was working out all the time to build strength and muscle, and, I think for the first time, she actually looked at me. I mean, saw me the way other girls do—the way I'm put together, down to the freckles on my arms and legs.

I cleared my throat self-consciously. Something had changed between us in that moment, because she seemed just as rattled as I, darting quick looks at me, then away.

She climbed into the car, carefully avoiding the chance to touch, and I went round to the driver's side. "So? What do you say? Got time for a cold drink?" I couldn't look at her because it mattered so much, what she'd say. There was so much I didn't know about her— from the simplest things, like the kind of music and movies and flavor of ice cream she liked, to what she thought about the future and the world . . . everything. But I wouldn't beg.

"Look, Cam. I'm sorry," she said with what sounded like genuine regret. "I'd love to go with you now, but I can't. I have to get home to shower and dress. I've got a party this afternoon and there's lots to do to get ready."

"Sure," I said, swallowing my disappointment. "Another time. I understand." But I didn't. It was only eleven o'clock in the morning. How long would it take to stop for a cold drink? How long could it take to get dressed for a party in the afternoon?

Silence, I guess, says a lot, because I pulled to the curb in front of Laurel's house and, without saying a word, handed over the rackets from the back seat.

She climbed out of the car, then stuck her head back in to say, "So long, Cam. It was fun. Tennis next week?"

"Sure."

"Well, great."

Staring straight ahead, with my hands gripping the steering wheel, I didn't realize what was happening until it was all over. She kneeled into the car on the seat beside me, and so quick it seemed almost as if it didn't happen, she kissed me.

7

I stood in front of the food table at Amy's party that evening holding a paper plate and looking over the goodies. Lots of chips and dips, rabbit food for the dieting girls, nuts, little meatballs in a hot sauce, deviled eggs, shrimp.

I was getting pretty good at figuring the calories and grams of protein without having to check a chart: 660 for a quart of whole milk, 33 protein; 400 for a half pound of steak, 46 protein; less than 10 for a single shrimp but almost 8 grams protein. I piled on the meatballs, two deviled eggs, lots of nuts for the carbohydrates, and some shrimp. I could hear Mike: "You gotta get 200 grams of protein a day." In my head he was always standing over me, watching, counting up the calories and grams of protein, no matter where I was.

"Leave some for the rest of us!" someone shouted in my ear.

"Hey, Kev! Where ya been?" I turned, raising my voice to be heard above the noise of the stereo and the voices around me. "These are good. Try one!" I skewered a meatball and popped it in his mouth.

"Didn't see you at practice Friday. Goofing off as usual?"

Kevin grinned and with a full mouth said, "Cooney gave me the boot. I am no longer on the team."

"Aw, Kev!" Someone jostled my arm and I nearly dropped the plate.

"No big deal. Who wants to play, anyway? Sure, it's fun being with the guys, but I don't have to play to do that."

"I'll talk to him," I said, moving away from the table.

"No! I wouldn't go back if he begged me on bended knee. What kind of guy is he anyway? Dumping me for a little pot when Reese is on coke? But of course, coke turns Reese into a raging bull . . . which makes all the difference!"

Beneath all his seeming indifference Kevin hurt bad. I could tell. We'd been in football together since freshman year. Most of our friends were on the team. If Cooney suddenly cut *me* out I'd feel lost, like an arm or leg had been whacked off.

"So what are you going to do, Kev?" It was too late to go into any other sport. To be good at track or baseball or basketball, you had to have started early. And now, without the discipline of practice, Kevin would have a lot more time on his hands. And for a guy like Kevin, that could mean trouble.

He swiped a deviled egg from my plate, tilted his head back, and dropped it into his mouth. "Who knows? Maybe I'll become a dealer." He brightened. "Why not? Make myself a million bucks before I'm eighteen. I'll sell to the guys! How about that? Create a team of zombies just to spite Cooney!"

I laughed with him. "And get twenty years. . . . Come on, Kev. Let's go find the girls and have some fun."

I wondered where Laurel spent her Saturday nights. If she didn't like guys in sports, then what kind did she like? Nerds? Did she go to movies and skating rinks and parties, like I did, like my friends did? I wondered now, as Kevin and I circulated, talking to Darcy or Erika or Tina from the pep squad, or James and Bruce from the team—just how Laurel might be spending this Saturday night. And with whom?

"Looking good, Potter. Real good!," Warren Brown announced, coming up from behind and punching me hard on the arm. "Mike sure knows his stuff, huh?"

"Sure does, Crunch," I said, using the team nickname for him and thinking what bad skin he had. His face was as broken out as if he feasted on chocolates all day, and he had an ugly habit of picking at the pustules while talking to someone. But what a build! He played defensive lineman and was as solid, as heavy, as strong as a tank. He could stop a guy with the slightest twist of a hip, and if he fell on you, you could be out for days.

We worked beside each other at Mike's a lot. Between exercises I'd see him pop a half dozen liver-plus tablets, other stuff too, maybe vitamins, maybe not. In six months, he told me, he'd put on forty pounds and was working to put on twenty more.

"See you're walking okay again," he said.

"Hey, Kev, wait!" I called as Kevin walked off with a casual flip of the hand. "Shoot!" I watched him thread his way through the dancers, heading, I figured, for the john, or another place where he could light up a joint in private. "Yeah, I'm okay again," I said, turning back to Crunch.

"You hear about Mike?"

"No. What?" I asked, searching around for where to put the empty plate. Amy was heading toward us, a small, thin girl in tow.

"He's in the hospital."

"Yeah?" A funny surge of fear shot through me. "What for?"

"Appendicitis."

"Appendicitis?"

"Yeah. Monty's taking over till he comes back."

"Gee," I said, as Amy sidled up and put a hand through my arm. "We should find out where he's at and visit him."

"Visit who?" Amy asked. Without waiting for my answer she said, "Listen, you guys, enough's enough. I've been watching you two. All you've done since you got here is eat and talk to other guys. Why do you think we invited you?"

"To eat and talk to other guys?"

"Warren," Amy said, ignoring me. "This is Sue. She's a new flag girl and she just *loves* football. I thought you might have a lot in common. Cam? Let's dance."

We edged into the family room, where the couches had been moved to the side, and joined the clot of dancers. A slow foxtrot was playing, and hardly moving on the crowded floor, we clung together, dancing cheek to cheek. I wondered why my hormones didn't act up. It didn't take much, usually, just close encounters like this, regardless of who was in my arms.

But nothing happened. Amy clung, fingers lightly stroking my neck, and I moved with the music. But absolutely nothing happened. I was beginning to wonder if the steroids had burned out my libido.

To hide my disinterest I got Amy talking, a pleasant sort of monologue that didn't take more than an occasional encouraging grunt from me to keep it going. She went on about losing a contact lens, about getting a new hairdo, about Cheryl and Kevin, and about some girl we both knew and her modeling job.

And then suddenly she asked, "Do you know Laurel Greene?"

Boy, if hormones had legs, I'd say mine were doing the boogaloo.

"Sure, I know her. Why?"

"Oh, nothing. She's going to Palm Springs next weekend. Luck-y. Wish I could."

The news hit me like an ice water shower. Even though she'd told me, in my head I'd already planned that Laurel would be at the game Friday. That she'd stick around and we'd go out later. That we'd play tennis again on Saturday. That . . . who knows. How would I ever get to know her if we could never get together?

Friday night we played Crescent Valley in their own home territory. Cooney had us arrive almost two hours early to warm up and for last-minute instructions. I really get wound up before a game. If I eat anything, it all comes up before the first play. I don't even like to talk to anybody or have anybody talk to me. Still, I missed having Kevin around. He was always so laid-back, and his crazy fooling around and dumb jokes somehow eased the tension.

Before we went out on the field Cooney gave us the usual pep talk. "You guys are going to win! Right?"

"Right!"

"Say it! Let me hear you. 'We're going to Win!' "

"We're going to Win!"

"What?" Cooney cupped a hand to his ear. "I didn't hear you!"

"We're going to Win!"

"Right! And you know *why*?"

"Why?" we asked in unison.

"Because you're the toughest! Because you're the meanest! Because you try the hardest! Because we've got the best passers and the best receivers and the best guards and the godawful meanest linebackers. Because you're the Best! That's why!"

As dumb as it sounds, it works. His words stir something in all of us that gets the adrenaline flowing, and we know as we jog out to the field that we'll do anything to prove what he says. Somehow, everything comes together. All the plays are written indelibly on our brains. We feel like the finest centurions going out to battle. We'll run our hearts out. We'll play though our lungs are exploding. We'll fight to stay in the game no matter how badly hurt or how great the pain.

Game time goes by like ten minutes. I'm hardly aware of the flag girls and the song girls and the cheerleaders and pep commissioners on the side waving their flags, singing their songs, jumping and cheering us on. All I'm conscious of is my job of getting that pigskin into the right hands, calling the right plays so we'll get a first down, and another, and a touchdown, and another.

Not until half time, when we were behind 10 to 7, sitting in the locker room, listening to Cooney read us the riot act, did I think about Laurel for an instant.

"Where were *you*, Reese?" he screamed at Tom, hands on hips. "You were supposed to stop Anderson! How the hell could you let him get by!" Reese lowered his head and I tuned out as he lit into one guy after another.

I was playing well, as well as I'd ever played. Amy would lavish me with praise for it. And Laurel didn't even care. She was away having fun in Palm Springs.

What a dismal weekend ahead. Even the party after the game had no appeal. I had it bad. All I wanted was Laurel. As I sat on the bench listening to Cooney's ranting, hating his guts, perspiring, slightly nauseous from hunger, anxious about the second half and wondering if we could pick up the lost points and still win—I had a sudden brilliant inspiration. Why wait for Monday to see her? Tomorrow, come what may, I'd get a bunch of guys together and we'd take the weekend off.

I smiled at the thought. And guess where we'd go?

8

We left the morning overcast and dismal chill of Los Angeles by nine, Kevin, Peter, and I, driving in Peter's red seven-year-old Toyota. Fifteen miles north of Palm Springs the sun burned out the fog and a clear, bright blue sky smiled down on us.

"This is more like it!" Kevin dug into the corn-chip bag and stuffed a handful in his mouth. "Now and then you come up with a good idea."

"So you lost the game," Peter said, lighting up a cigarette.

"Ten to seven. We just couldn't get going that last quarter. What we needed was Kev—"

"Yeah. Ha ha. Tell that to Cooney," Kevin said.

"Ten miles more." I sighed. How in the world would I find Laurel in a city of maybe five hundred motels? My game plan called for getting on the phone and calling the places most of the kids we knew stayed at, which could take hours. And what if she was staying at a private home?

Kevin passed me a Baggie-wrapped sandwich, which I tore open with my teeth while checking the rearview mirror. A yellow convertible dogged our rear, trying to pass.

"Hey hey," Peter announced quietly, winding down the window on his side. "What have we here?"

The car pulled even and I tried to sneak looks at the girls in the front seat while eating the sandwich and driving.

Peter stuck his head and shoulders out of the car window. "Hi, there, gorgeous," he called. "Where you staying? Get together tonight for some fun?"

As the convertible passed, the dark-haired girl beside the driver turned and kneeled on the front seat so she could look back at us. I whistled appreciatively. She wore a flowered bikini that barely covered anything. Smiling, she waved, blew us a kiss, then gave us the finger before settling back in her seat.

We all laughed, especially Peter. When we'd left L.A. his mood had been as gray as the weather. He hated spending money—saving it, I suppose, for that day when he could take a place of his own. He was torn between staying home and earning overtime, or coming with us and parting with some hard-earned bucks.

We ran down all the windows as we came into town and slowed to a crawl because of the heavy traffic. I was in no hurry. I loved the lazy feel of the place, the people strolling the broad streets window-shopping, looking each other over, licking ice cream cones. I loved it all— the older buildings with purple bougainvillea climbing their walls and spilling onto rooftops; the hot, dry, pungent air; the bright sky overhead. It made me feel great —happy and carefree.

"So what do you say, guys?" Kevin asked. "Do we

stop and have lunch now, or check in first and swim before lunch?"

"Lunch now," I said. "I'm still hungry."

"May as well," Peter agreed. "We can't get the room until after two anyway. Say!" he exclaimed, suddenly excited. "Isn't that the yellow convertible we saw on the way in? It is! There they are! Hey, Cam, turn here! Hurry! Maybe we can get something going for tonight!"

I swerved left to get off the main drag, where parking was impossible, and found a parking space within the first block, a good omen. As soon as I parked, Pete and Kevin sprinted off to find the girls. "Meet you at Hamburger Hamlet in twenty minutes," Kevin called back over his shoulder. "Wish us luck!"

I locked the car and put some coins in the meter, then ambled off to the main street. Pete and Kevin appeared to have made contact in front of a bookstore and were deep in conversation, so I passed on by. I browsed in an art shop, checked some sale tapes outside a record store, and then stood at the back of a small crowd of kids and their parents, near a toy store, watching a clown. The performer sported a large red nose, a head of moplike orange hair, and a red and white polka-dot suit. He, or she, blew up long, slender balloons and deftly bent and looped, twisted, knotted, and tied them into dogs and giraffes, flowers, and even people, then gave each to a child. I couldn't take my eyes away.

"She's terrific," a woman nearby exclaimed, though as far as I could tell the clown could as well have been male with its baggy clothes and exaggerated makeup.

Presently she, or he, gave her last creation to one of

the many outstretched hands and untied a loosely knotted bouquet of helium balloons from a chair. A cry of stunned surprise broke from the crowd, as, through pantomime, the clown appeared to rise above the ground, fighting gravity. It was so real that even I gasped, wanting to reach out and save her from floating away.

And then something strange happened. My heart began to thump for no apparent reason. My throat tightened as something familiar about the clown's eyes made me think of Laurel. Impossible, my brain said. You're crazy. But once the idea took root it wouldn't go away, and I moved closer, looking for some telling clue to confirm my feeling.

"Do an elephant!" someone in the crowd called. And with almost no effort the clown became a lumbering pachyderm, head swaying ponderously as if slowed by its unwieldy trunk, legs shuffling slowly.

"Do a drunk! Do a kangaroo! Do a cat!"

I swallowed the lump in my throat and watched, entranced. If only she'd speak. Maybe her voice would give her away. But finally she bowed to the crowd and began to pack away her equipment. The crowd slowly dispersed, moving into the toy shop or down the street.

"Laurel?" I asked softly.

She swung around and our eyes connected. There was recognition and surprise, and a bolt of electricity crossed the space between us. If she was blushing, I could never tell through the thick makeup.

"Fancy meeting you here," I said to forestall any question about how come *I* was in Palm Springs.

"Yes, fancy," she said, a faint enigmatic smile already replacing the startled expression of a moment before. "How did you know it was me?" She began folding the chair and moving the helium cylinder out of foot traffic.

"Instinct."

"Ha." She shot me a disbelieving glance while she stuffed the remaining balloons into a bag.

"Let me help. Do these go inside?" I lifted the helium tank and chair and waited for her directions.

"I can do it!" she exclaimed as if she hated taking any help from me.

"I'm sure you can, a good strong woman like you," I said, waiting for her to lead the way. "How about lunch? I know a terrific Mexican restaurant near here."

"Thanks, but I have work to do. I go on again in twenty minutes."

"Tonight then? You don't have to work tonight, do you?"

She hesitated for long enough for me to think that if she turned me down again, that was it. It was dumb chasing after someone who gave you so little encouragement. "Well, okay—sure," she said at last, as if she'd been having an argument with herself. "Why not?" Her oversized clown lips curled in a smile.

I suppressed the urge to jump up and down and instead wrote down where she was staying (a relative's home), and set the time for picking her up.

When I left the store, it felt as if *my* feet weren't touching the ground. I looked back, hoping she'd be watching, but Laurel was already surrounded by a school of little children, passing out lollipops.

* * *

"Now that's silly," I argued with Kevin and Peter. "There's no reason we can't all have dinner together. I told her I was here with you two. She'll expect it."

Peter shook his head. "Look, kid brother. I didn't come to Palm Springs to spend the evening with someone else's date. We'll be fine. In fact, the girls told us about two parties we can crash, right here at the motel, and another two blocks away. So don't worry about us. You can even take the car. Have a ball."

"Kev?" I asked, wondering if my brother was just being nice.

"You heard him." Kevin licked the side of his ice cream cone. "Actually, he's relieved. Less competition. Right, Pete?" He dodged Peter's punch.

And so, several hours later, dressed in white chinos and a blue polo shirt, I went to pick up Laurel.

The home she was staying at was near the Palm Springs Racquet Club, one of the fancier parts of town. If there's one thing that ties my tongue, it's being outclassed. Anything can do it. Someone who beats the pants off me on the playing field. Someone who's a lot smarter or has a better sense of humor. Guys with money.

Knocking at the door of that big, modern house that must have cost in the million range, I felt very much the poor kid from the other side of the tracks. Unsure of myself and what I had to offer, shy. Fortunately, Laurel answered the door, saving me from having to go through the Mr. Nice Guy act for her relatives.

"You look . . . super," I said as Laurel came toward me, wearing a white sundress and carrying a green jacket.

"Thanks," she said, with that wonderful secret smile that made my knees buckle. "I considered leaving the clown makeup on, but I didn't want to embarrass you."

"You couldn't do that," I said, helping her into the car. "But you'd surely raise a few eyebrows where we're going."

"Where's that?"

I told her the name of the steak house where I'd made reservations—and where it would take a big hunk of my earnings for the next two weeks to pay the tab.

"Unh-unh," she announced, firmly, as I settled into the driver's seat. "Unless you want to go dutch. And *I* don't want to spend that kind of money. I work too hard to earn it."

"That's nice of you to worry about my wallet, but forget it. I *asked* you. We don't go dutch."

"Now listen, Cam," she said, facing me, arms folded. "Let's be straight with each other. I don't measure a guy by how much he spends on me. That place is expensive. You don't have to do that!"

"I know I don't! I want to!"

"Well, I don't. We go someplace where you don't have to trade your soul to feed me, or I stay home. Which is it?"

"I don't know whether to be insulted or impressed. You're the first girl who's ever objected to how much I spent on her."

"Be impressed."

We ended up at a nice Italian restaurant with white tablecloths and soft music playing in the background. Laurel really liked it. She gazed appreciatively at the murals of the Colosseum, of fountains and gardens, a smile of pleasure on her face. "So tell me, how do you happen to be in Palm Springs?" she asked.

"I wanted to see you, of course. Why else?" Man, it made me feel good, sitting opposite her. Her laughter reminded me of small bells tinkling. I felt unbelievably happy, and totally turned on.

"Oh sure! You drove a hundred miles to see me, not even knowing where I'd be staying."

"I did!" I protested, laughing at her disbelief. "Believe me! You promised me a tennis lesson this week. Right? So, I'm here to take you up on it."

"You're either crazy or very inventive!" When she laughed her eyes did too. "Come on. What's the real reason?" I had to look away for fear she'd see how strongly I felt.

Fortunately the waiter came by then to leave menus and a wood plank with a loaf of hot bread. I pretended to be very interested in the menu while she waited for my answer.

"Okay. So there was another reason," I said after a while, thinking hard for a reason she'd accept. "Kevin has been cut from the football team. This weekend is sort of a consolation prize."

"Oh, I'm sorry! Why was he cut? Isn't it rather late in the season for that?"

"Uh-huh." I picked up the knife and sliced the bread, offering it first to Laurel, then taking two slices for myself. "When Kevin's under pressure he gets pretty uptight. And Cooney puts a lot of pressure on us. So to cope, Kev smokes a little pot. Not that much . . . but, you know. And Cooney doesn't like it, so he threw him out."

"You think Cooney was unfair?"

"I sure do. Cooney allows, even condones, other things—like coke—and . . ." I hesitated, and buttered the bread so I wouldn't have to look at her, "and steroids . . . so it seems pretty hypocritical."

"But—but that's awful! Why?"

I busied myself eating and asked, "Why what?"

"Why would anyone risk his health by taking drugs? Football just isn't that important. Nothing is!"

"Steroids aren't drugs. They're hormones," I corrected.

"Drugs—hormones, what's the difference? They're both bad."

"You don't understand," I said. "Football is a big thing in our school, in the whole country. You learn a lot when you compete, like discipline, like always trying to be better than you were yesterday. And it carries over into other things. Winning is important. Some guys would do anything to win."

"Would you?"

Her question startled me. I stopped playing with the crumb on my plate and looked up at her. "Sure. Why not? I've got a chance to win scholarships at some of the best schools in the country because of football. My father would be so proud he'd announce it from the top of City Hall! Sure, I'd do anything!"

"Anything?"

I shrugged. "Oh, come on. You know what I mean."

"I don't think so. I mean, aside from the fact that that stuff can't be good for you, what about the ethics? What about the fact that it's not fair sportsmanship?" There was a closed look to her face, like the first night we'd talked, as if she'd already decided I wasn't worth knowing.

Darn, I thought. *How'd I get into this? Things were going so well and now I've ruined everything.*

"Laurel, you don't know what you're talking about," I said. Somehow she had a way of always throwing me off balance. "Everyone is looking for that extra edge to make him better than the next guy."

"Would you like to order now?" the smiling waiter asked, standing above us and saving me from making matters worse.

"Laurel?" I picked up the menu and pretended to study it again.

Laurel bent toward me when the waiter left, expecting me to go on. But what could I tell her? That sure, I was on steroids? That other guys on other teams used it too? She had no idea of the kind of pressure guys are under to win. Amy would understand. Amy would never question what I was doing. She knew the score. Anything to win. But Laurel? Never.

Unfortunately, it wasn't Amy I cared about.

So instead of elaborating, I shrugged and, putting on my most disarming smile, reached for Laurel's hand. "Let's talk about you for a change," I said. "Tell me all about this clown stuff. How did you get started? What's it like? How long have you been at it? How come you didn't tell me you were so great?"

"Cam," she replied, withdrawing her hand. "*You* wouldn't take coke or steroids, would you?"

My face burned at the question. "Are you kidding?"

She watched my face for a moment, then took a deep breath. "Then you're *not.* Good. For a minute there, I wasn't sure." She picked up her fork and speared a hunk of salad.

What could I say? If I told the truth, she'd lose all respect for me, so I didn't confirm or deny. She was an idealist. She didn't have the faintest understanding of the real world of sports.

She put down her fork and leaned forward. her face took on an expression of joy and her voice became animated. "Okay. Now let me tell you about being a clown," she said.

9

Sunday morning I slipped out of the room before Kevin or Peter awoke to get in some laps in the motel pool. And to think.

The evening with Laurel had been very special. After dinner I'd deliberately avoided parking near the busy streets in town where all you could do was window-shop and drove instead to a small playground where we could walk around and talk. Moonlight lit the wet lawn and the grass smelled newly mown.

"Race you," Laurel announced, slipping off her shoes so they wouldn't get wet. With a laugh of triumph she sprinted off toward the play area. By the time I'd undone my shoes she'd reached the canvas swings, dropped onto a seat, and was already pumping away.

"Hah!" she called out when I limped up, a pebble embedded in my foot. "Some jock you are, letting a girl beat you!"

"Ever think of going out for the track team?" I asked, climbing on the swing beside her.

We swung together side by side for a long time, talking, singing songs, swapping stories about our childhood. Just when I'd think she liked me, she'd react to something I said in such a funny way, a negative way, that I'd pull back, not sure what I'd said wrong. It was as if she could see right inside of me to all the faults and weaknesses, doubts and lacks that others never saw.

When it was time to go I slid off my swing and held out my arms to catch her as she flew out of hers. For one moment in time as I held her, I could smell the fresh lemony scent of her hair, feel her heart pounding against my ribs. I wanted to kiss her so badly I could hardly stand it. Oddly, I thought she wanted that too. But with a strange, strangled sound, and with gentle but firm force, she pulled away. I stared after her, heart still pounding, rattled, confused, while she gathered up her shoes and, turning back to me, held out a hand.

Sunbathers start early in Palm Springs. By the time I came out to do my pool laps the chairs and lounges were filling with visitors marking their territories for the day or already laid out for their ultraviolet fix. I found Pete and Kevin spread-eagled on chaises when I finished my laps, looking half alive. A pitcher of juice sat on the table beside them and sections of the Sunday paper.

Pete looked up, shielding his bloodshot eyes from the bright light, and fixed me with an envious gaze. "Umm-umm! You sure are something, kid brother. Not even a pimple. Laurel must have been all over that manly bod last night."

Kevin opened one eye a slit, groaned, and covered his face with a towel. "If she was, he probably couldn't do a thing about it."

"Looking a little green around the gills there, buddy," I said, reaching for the Baggie I'd left beside my towel. I poured myself a glass of juice and counted out the pills. "Is that green from last night or is it envy?" I popped the first three pills into my mouth and washed them down with juice.

Pete raised his head like a turtle coming out of its shell. "When are you going to stop taking those things?" he asked.

"When I reach my target weight." I chucked the remaining pills into my mouth.

"Do you ever stop to think what's happening inside you from that poison?"

"So how are the Red Sox doing?" I asked, picking up the sports section.

Sure I wondered what the steroids were doing. I checked my privates every day to see if they had shrunk. I checked the mirror all the time for the telltale bad skin or yellow pallor. As for the blood pressure, I didn't know. So maybe it went up a little, even a lot, but at seventeen, I couldn't imagine having a stroke.

"There's an interesting article on page two," Pete said.

"Yeah, what?"

He lay on his stomach on the chaise looking like a beached whale. "Read it."

I turned to page two and checked the headlines. Halfway down the page on the right was an article about an NFL player who said he'd been taking anabolic steroids for six years until he began to notice back pains. The steroids had nearly destroyed his kidneys.

I threw the sports section back on the table. "Anyone see the comics?"

"No comment?"

"Lay off, Pete!"

Kevin raised the towel from his eyes. "Yeah, Pete. Half the guys in the NFL are on something. Nice guys finish last."

"'To quote some poet whose name escapes me," Pete replied, "when the One Great Scorer comes to write against your name, he marks—not that you won or lost —but how you played the game.'"

"Cute," I said, not letting on that he'd hit a nerve. It wasn't the effect of steroids on my body that bothered me so much; I sort of felt immortal. No, that wasn't it. Pete had hit on the one thing that really ate away at my conscience. The morality issue.

I'm a pretty straight guy. I don't crib answers on exams. When a salesperson gives me too much change I give it back. I'm no angel, but I'm a fair fighter, a pretty honest guy all around. Until lately. Now I was playing with a stacked deck. And it didn't feel good.

Kevin sat up. "Oh *yeah*! Kee-*yute*!" he said, repeating my word but referring instead to the two girls letting themselves into the pool area. *"Mamma mia!* I'll take the redhead!"

Pete sat up, all interest. I melted back into the shade of the umbrella, glad the attention had shifted from me. With a sense of dismay I knew that getting the scholarship mattered more to me at this moment than my health, than my sense of sportsmanship, more even than Laurel's opinion of me.

* * *

"When's Mike coming back?" I asked Monty the next time I checked in at the gym. Crunch was pumping away on the stationary bike and eyeing a chick on the mat.

"Good going," Monty said, writing down my weight on the record sheet Mike kept. Without looking up he said, "No telling about Mike. These things can take a while."

"My brother had appendicitis when he was fifteen. He was in the hospital for maybe five days. Playing ball in two weeks."

Monty tapped the pencil on the clipboard. His gray eyes met mine. "That so?"

"Where's he at?" I asked, wrapping a towel around my shoulders. "Thought I might look in on him some evening."

"He's at Huntington, but I don't think he's ready for company. Why don't you wait a while. Now go inside and warm up, then call me. I want to change your routine this week, increase the weights, do a little more to build the laterals."

I didn't think of Mike again until several days later after football practice. It had been one of those days when Cooney didn't like anything anyone did. He spent the last half hour of practice ripping into Crunch. "What's the matter with you, mister? You got lead in your pants today?" He rapped a fist against his head. "You got cotton candy up here?" Referring to Crunch's constant gum chewing, he said, "If you kept your feet as busy as that mouth of yours, maybe you wouldn't have looked like such a shit out there today!"

He wasn't going to put up with anyone not giving his

best, he said. He wouldn't put up with stupidity or laziness, or lateness, or back talk, and most of all he wouldn't put up with *losing.* And before he dismissed us we had to run fifteen extra laps. We left the gym too tired to care, dispirited, but scared enough of Cooney's anger to know that somehow we'd have to work even harder.

It was later that evening, after dinner, that I thought about Mike again. I was sitting at my desk, trig book open, pencil in hand, paper in front of me, and the mind blank. I felt hyped up, yet tired, physically wired, but without the mental energy to face the homework assignment. I went into the kitchen and downed a glass of milk. I stopped in Pete's room to talk, but he wasn't there. Finally, looking for anything to postpone having to concentrate, I decided to phone the hospital and find out about Mike.

"Mike Taft's room, please," I said to the operator.

"One moment." Pause. And then she said, "Sorry, he's not taking calls yet. He's in intensive care."

"Intensive care?" I asked, surprised. It must have been a week since he'd been admitted. What was he doing in intensive care? Appendicitis was no big deal! "Can you tell me his condition?"

"I'll be glad to connect you with I.C.," the operator said.

"Please." I held the receiver tight against my ear.

"Intensive Care Unit. Nurse Ramirez speaking," the next voice said. "May I help you?"

"I wonder if you can tell me how Mike Taft is doing," I said.

"Are you family?"

I thought for a minute about lying, but said, "No. Just a friend."

The nurse must have referred to some records and then said, "He's stable—as well as can be expected at this point."

"At this point? What do you mean? Were there complications?"

"I'm sorry, I'm not at liberty to say. You might speak to his family."

"But . . . but . . ." I stammered, and then realized there was no use in going on. "When he's awake, would you please tell him Cam Potter called?"

"Will do," the nurse said.

I thanked her and hung up, then stared at the phone for a long time. What was wrong with Mike? Why was he in intensive care? Was he going to be all right?

10

"Well, well!" Pete greeted one evening, coming into the kitchen. He leaned against the doorframe, tapped a cigarette out of a pack, and grinned. "What have we here? Gorging on forbidden fruit, are we? What will Cooney say?"

I stopped midway in chewing off a big hunk of bologna with white bread, oozing mayonnaise, and grinned sheepishly. "Want some?" I held out a half empty package of potato chips. As long as I was going to sabotage my diet, I might as well go whole hog. After a month of high protein, high carbohydrate foods, I had a right—a need—an absolute hunger—to pig out. "It's not going to hurt," I said, mouth full.

"But all those *fats*! All that *salt*! All that *red dye*! Tch, tch!" He shook his head in dismay. "Cooney's gonna take one look at you Monday and blow a fuse!"

"Oh, shut up!" I flexed my muscles. "Look at me! Not an ounce of fat. Great definition! I've put on eighteen pounds. One little feast like this won't kill me."

"Well, you better not take any chances," Pete said, serious now. He picked up an ashtray and brought it to the table. "If you really want to go to college, you better find a way to pay for it yourself, because Dad can't help. He's inside doing the books. He's trying to figure out how he can afford a new truck; the old one needs tires, and the transmission's gone gaflooey." He took a long drag on his cigarette. "And I'm going to put another kink in the works."

I quit chewing and looked up. "Yeah, what?"

"I'm quitting." He paused, waiting for my reaction.

"You're kidding!"

"I kid you not."

"When?"

"End of the month."

"Oh, wow! What are you going to do?"

"I met a couple of guys. One of them has contacts in construction in Santa Barbara. We're going to form our own company. One guy does landscaping. Another does driveways and walks. I know the sprinkler business. They want me to go out and bid the jobs." Pete's eyes brightened. He sat straighter.

I whistled. "You tell Dad yet?"

"Nope."

I thought about it for a moment and, without thinking, reached for Pete's cigarettes. "He'll be furious!"

"I know. And that's not all."

I glanced toward the doorway, knowing Mom and Dad were nearby, wondering if they could hear.

"I'm moving out. Jason is renting a big house in Santa Barbara. It would be crazy, commuting from here. He's letting me stay with him, rent-free for a while—just until I start paying my way."

"Gosh, Pete. Are you sure? It's so risky. Look how hard it is for Dad."

Pete stubbed out his cigarette in the ashtray, reached for another, and then put it back. "Sure it's risky. But it's time I cut the cord. Dad thinks I'm an idiot." He shook his head and waved me to silence as I began to object. "It's my life. Why should anyone else tell me how to live it? Sure, I'm scared. Maybe I am an idiot. But maybe not. I want to find out."

I reached across the table and gripped Pete's shoulder. "I'm going to miss you like crazy."

"Gonna miss you. Gonna miss the old man too. Funny thing is, I love him." He got a funny, crooked smile on his face. "But I gotta do what's best for me now. It's time." Pete's hand shook as he reached for his matches. "Do me a favor?"

"Sure, what?" I put the unlit cigarette down and pushed the chair back.

"I haven't the guts to face them alone. Come in with me now when I tell Dad?"

"You're what?" Dad cried, half rising from the dining room chair, hands flat on the table.

Pete stepped back as if he'd been slapped.

"You ungrateful—! After all I've done for you? If it weren't for me, where would you be? And what a time to bail out! When I need you most!"

"Bill, please," Mom pleaded. "Pete's always tried his best. You're just upset over the books."

"How's he gonna manage, huh?" Dad asked, turning to Mom. "He'll starve out there in the real world! How can he do this? I teach him all I know. I give him a good salary. All I ask in return is loyalty—and what do I get? He's the first one to leave the sinking ship!"

"Come on, honey. Don't exaggerate. You've had bad times before," Mom said.

"When did you ever say you needed me, Dad?" Pete asked, face flushed. "Come on. Be honest. I work hard. I do everything you ask, and all you ever do is criticize me. You make me feel like you're doing me a favor to keep me on. So, fine. I'm doing you a favor. I'm leaving!"

"Good. So leave! See if I care. You can leave tonight. Just pack up your things and go!" Dad nodded toward me. "You haven't got an ounce of Cam's guts. So, go!"

"Hey, Dad, *please!*" I cried. "Stop it! Don't pit us against each other! Pete's not trying to hurt you. Don't be like that! Let him go. Tell him it's okay!"

Dad slammed the account book closed and rose from his chair, almost knocking it over. "So you're against me too!" he cried. "Sure. I'll give him my blessing! Go ahead, leave me. Good luck. But if you fail, don't come crying back to me!"

"I won't!" Pete shouted. "Don't worry. I won't! Not if my life depends on it!"

I watched Dad hurry out of the dining room, eyes fixed straight ahead. Mom raised her hands in despair and dropped them. "Don't let him get to you, Pete. You know your father. You just caught him at a bad time, that's all. He's very upset that we can't afford a new truck right now. He's not himself. He'll come around."

"He's *never* really cared about me, Mom!" Pete's face had turned the color of putty and he seemed to have shrunk into himself. "I don't care if he ever comes around!"

"Oh, honey. That's not true! Don't say that!" Mom cried.

"It is true, Mom," I said. "I don't know how Pete's taken it this long. I'm surprised he doesn't hate me, the way Dad ignores him and sets me up as some kind of white knight." I swallowed the big lump in my throat. "Pete's terrific. I think he's got a lot of guts, doing what he's doing."

"Please, Pete," Mom begged, not even hearing what I said. "Wait until tomorrow. Tomorrow he'll feel different. Don't leave tonight. Not this way. Your father loves you. I know he does."

"No, Mom." Pete mumbled. "I can't. Not the way he feels." He walked over to Mom and put his arms around her. "I'll be around. Don't worry. Maybe you and Cam will come visit."

I helped Pete pack, a rock in my throat for the pain he was feeling and for the loss I was already feeling. It should have been a happy time. After all, he was starting a new life and he was scared, but he was excited too. We didn't talk about the argument with Dad, but it hung between us like a barbed-wire fence. Instead, we talked of the good times. I reminded him of how awkward I was as a kid, how he was the one taught me to throw a ball, to ride a bike, to deal with bullies. I couldn't imagine what it would be like without him around.

"Okay, little brother," he said, after the last box had been loaded in his car. "I'm on my way." He glanced back at the lighted windows of the house for a long moment and shrugged. "Wish me luck."

"You know I do."

He knuckled me on the shoulder and then we hugged hard and quickly. "Take care of yourself, kid. And if you need me, you know where I'll be." He climbed in the Toyota, took one last look at the house, and drove away.

The house became a funeral home with Pete gone. It didn't make sense that one person's absence could make such a difference, but the family balance had changed. I missed Pete's whistling, the wet towels he left in the bathroom, the late-night talks when he'd come into my room with a beer, a jar of peanut butter and box of crackers. I missed the joking that went on at mealtimes between us, and the easy conversation. My eyes kept jumping to his empty chair. Although Mom said Dad asked *her* about Pete, at mealtimes he never mentioned him and concentrated all his conversation on me.

"You're looking great, Cam. Strong, like a bull. Like those big NFL players who take steroids!" He laughed and I tensed.

"How's it going at school?"

"Fine." Here we go with the nightly interrogation, I thought.

"How much weight you gain?"

"Twenty pounds."

"Hear from State yet?"

"No! Will you stop asking me the same questions every night!"

"Don't be so smart, young man. You're still living under my roof, eating from my table. I'll ask whatever I want to ask and you'll answer with a civil tongue or you can . . ."

"What? Or you'll throw me out?" I threw the napkin on the table and jumped up. "What kind of father are you? Have you talked to Pete since he moved out, huh? Do you only love us if we do exactly what you ask? What kind of father are you?"

"You button your mouth, mister! I've had just about enough of that! You're getting too smart for your own good. What's the matter? You think once you get a scholarship you won't need your old parents anymore, huh? Sure. Just like that brother of yours."

"I give up." I turned to Mom. She looked like she might cry. "I'm sorry, Mom. I'm not hungry anymore."

"You come back here, you hear? Cam? You come back and finish your dinner! Cam! You hear me?" Dad screamed as I ran out of the dining room.

I slammed the door to my room and found myself grinding my teeth in a clenched jaw. I had all this repressed energy with no way to release it. I wanted to pound my fists against the wall, to hurl a chair across the room, to tear the bedclothes off the bed. I stalked around growling like an animal, wanting to scream, to hit someone, and then I grabbed a jacket and ran out of the house.

11

"Cam!" Laurel exclaimed, opening the door to me. She was wearing jeans and a long sweater.

"Can you come for a walk?"

She checked her watch. "It's late. I have a report to finish. You could have phoned!"

"Can you come for a walk?" I felt so hyper I wanted to grab her by the arm and yank her away.

She must have seen something in my face, something desperate, because she said, "Wait. I'll get my jacket." In a moment she was back, and the two of us walked out to the street, hands in the pockets of our jackets against the November chill.

"What's wrong?" she asked as we passed houses still decorated with pumpkins for Halloween.

I poured it all out in one long stream of words. About Pete's leaving, and Dad, and how I couldn't even stand working for him anymore. And how I realized that Dad probably felt a failure because his business wasn't going well and because Pete left, which he saw as another failure on his part, but that it was no reason for him to disown one son and make life miserable for the other.

She let me go on and on, without interrupting, and when I was finished, I just stopped.

"Feel better?"

"Yes. Not that getting it all out changes anything."

"You want to know what I think?" Fog blurred the streetlights, made her presence beside me seem unreal.

I nodded and took her arm.

"I think you overreacted. Your father is under a lot of pressure if his business isn't going well. He overreacted to your brother. And you're overreacting to your dad's pitiful efforts to make conversation." She raised a hand as I started to object. "I said 'pitiful' because I'll bet since Pete left you've had it in for your dad. I'll bet you've done everything you can to punish him. Like clamming up at mealtime?" She looked at me and nodded. "Aha. I was right. So take some of the blame yourself. At least *he* 'tried.' "

"Shoot!" I exploded, dropping her arm. "That's the most simplistic psychobabble I ever heard."

"So don't pay me the five cents."

We walked apart in an uncomfortable silence while I mulled over what she'd said. I guessed there was more than a little truth to it. But knowing that didn't make me feel any better. I still felt angry, resentful, full of a mean energy looking for something or someone to spend it on.

"I've got to get home," Laurel said. "That report is due tomorrow and I have a lot more to do."

"So let it wait!"

"Maybe *you* don't get reports in on time, but I do!" She about-faced and strode back down the street toward her house.

I caught up with her in two strides in a darker section of the street and swung her around by the shoulders. "I've been wanting to do this ever since I met you," I said, bringing her into the circle of my arms. I held her in a vise grip and before she knew what was coming, planted a kiss on her lips. Not the tender kiss I fantasized about when I went to sleep at night, but a hard, brutal, hurtful kiss that gave me no pleasure and surely gave her less.

With all the strength she had she pushed me away, stood back, and wiped her mouth as if she had just tasted something awful. "You . . . you . . . *jock!*" she cried. "Don't you ever try that again!" Even in the poor light before she ran off, I could see the tears in her eyes, the contempt.

Ei-yi-yi, I thought, striking a fist into the palm of my other hand again and again. "What's the matter with me? What have I done now? I've ruined everything!"

Kevin's home is only three blocks from mine. That's where I ran after I made sure—from a distance—that Laurel got home safely. Not to cry on his shoulder, but to put a little space between what had just happened and facing up to what a bastard I really was.

"He's in his room," Kevin's mother said, wrapping a blue robe around her legs. Her eyes were bloodshot. She'd been drinking. I could smell it even three feet away.

"I won't stay long!" I brushed by her to the door that led to the basement play room and Kevin's living quarters.

"Hey, man!" Kevin raised one hand in a lazy greeting. He was lying on the couch, smoking a joint. The TV was on to a game show, the images flickering but the sound off. "What's up?"

"Just passing," I said, sniffing the air. A guy could get stoned just breathing in that room.

"So sit." Kevin closed his eyes and took a deep inhale, then held the joint out to me.

"No thanks."

"Oh, right." He withdrew his hand and smiled. "No pot. Just little blue pills, right?"

"Right."

Kevin closed his eyes again and lay back on the pillow, really zonked.

"Hey, I wanna talk! Don't go to sleep on me!"

"Talk. I'm listening." The phone on the end table near Kevin rang. I jumped. He opened his eyes and slowly reached for the receiver.

"Yeah, it's me," he said, and then listened for a long time. "Yeah, sure. Third period. Same amount?" He listened, smiled at me with that same faraway look. "You know the price. No, I can't. Yes or no?" He nodded, hung up, and lay back against the pillows.

"Kev? You *dealing*?"

Kevin sighed contentedly.

I shook him. "Kev! I thought you were kidding before. Are you dealing?"

Kevin tried to struggle out of my grasp.

I let him fall back and stood over him, furious. "Damn you! You'll wind up in jail! Don't be stupid! It's one thing to smoke a little pot; it's another to deal! You're hooked, man! You're always zonked. I can hardly talk to you anymore. There's never anyone home!" I tapped my head to show him what I meant.

Kevin chuckled. He was too far out of it to care. I stood there, wanting to take him by the shoulders and shake some sense into him. Not knowing what to do.

But what was the use?

I left Kevin's house and just walked. Walked past the little park near Laurel's home. Past the dark buildings of the high school, the empty football field where dead leaves swirled in a dervishlike dance. And wound up back at Laurel's house, staring up at the lighted windows, wondering which was hers. And if she was still awake, stewing over what I'd done. And if she'd ever want to talk with me again.

Back home, I downed the last of the day's vitamins and steroids, and picked up the phone to call Pete.

"Hey, man," Pete answered, sleepily. "Do you know what time it is?"

"A little after eleven."

"A little before midnight, you mean. Do you know what time I get up? I work for a living, remember?"

"Okay. Okay." I could hear the belligerence in my tone. "So good-bye."

"Hey, wait a minute! Don't go away. As long as you woke me up, talk." He yawned. "What's up?"

"I just called to see how things are going."

He yawned again. "Just fine. I don't have any furniture yet and I'm living out of a suitcase and bedding down in a sleeping bag, but there's work coming in and I'm having a ball."

"The house is a morgue with you gone."

Pete hesitated, then said, "I miss you too, fella."

My throat got scratchy. "Got any room up there for a kid brother?"

"Anytime. How about this weekend?"

"How about tonight?"

"Hey, come on, Cam. What's going on?" He sounded fully awake now.

"I don't know. Nothing. Everything! Dad's going after *me* now that you're gone. There's supposed to be a narc on campus and Kevin's heading for some real bad trouble. And that's not all. I didn't even feel horny, but I got physical with Laurel tonight and she told me off."

"Maybe she's frigid," Pete said.

"No! No! I deserved everything she said. I don't know, Pete. Everything's piling up. I feel like punching out the whole goddam world!"

There was silence on the line and then Pete asked, "You think maybe it's the steroids?"

"Nah. How could it be? At least two other guys on the team are taking it, *and* Mike Taft. I don't see *them* throwing tantrums."

"Maybe you should see a doctor."

"And have him take blood tests? No way!"

"You've painted yourself into a corner, pal," Pete said. "I don't have any answers for you. Anyway, I'm not firing on all cylinders right now and I have to go to work in a few hours. What say we talk about this when you get up here?"

The digital clock on my dresser read twelve ten. "Yeah."

"How's Mom?" Pete asked.

"Okay." I waited, but he didn't ask about Dad.

Pete cleared his throat. "So, good night. I mean, good morning."

"Right."

"Be sure to let me know when you're coming up."

When I hung up, I dropped onto my bed, clamped my hands behind my head, and stared up at the ceiling. Tomorrow—today, rather—we were playing Glendale High. Coach said for everyone to get a good night's sleep, that if we didn't win this one, he'd have our hides.

Well, there wasn't much left of the night to sleep. But it didn't matter anyway. The way I felt, I had enough energy to win the game single-handed, right now.

12

The first period Monday morning is English. I got to class early hoping to catch Laurel before she went in, hoping to find the right words to patch things up. But hanging around the door is a bad place. Everyone stops and has something to say. Amy, for instance, had to discuss the scores of the opposing team we'd be playing today. She also liked to stand where she could be noticed when she wore her cheerleader outfit, a short gold skirt and red sweater, white sneaks and red and gold socks. Penny Dravinski had to rap, too, gazing up at me with such adoring eyes I wanted to run. Others, too, until a small circle of girls had me pinned against the wall while my eyes wandered above them, looking for Laurel.

"Excuse me, ladies. I have to see someone," I said as soon as I spotted her. I broke through the human wall and strode down the hall. "Look, I've got to talk to you a minute . . ." I tried to take Laurel's arm to turn her out of the hallway traffic. "Please."

"Let go!" Fire burned in her eyes. Guys flowed around us, checking out the drama. I dropped her arm fast, but blocked the way.

"I won't let you go until you hear me out," I said, lowering my voice.

"That figures, Mr. Strongarm." She stepped to one side to move ahead. I sidestepped to block her way.

"Look, I'm *sorry*. It was stupid, what I did. I'm sorry. It won't happen again."

"Darn right it won't!" She looked me straight in the eye. "I don't go for caveman tactics. I don't like being mauled. Nobody treats me like an object. Nobody! Now, please. Out of my way."

"Laurel!" I pleaded, as she swept by and strode into the room, past Amy and Penny, past others in our class who were getting an eyeful.

I forced a smile but felt like shoving everyone out of the way, like bellowing my pain. My whole life seemed to be falling apart. I took my seat and stared at my books, not once glancing in Laurel's direction. Not hearing a word the teacher spoke. Cooney's voice sounded in my head, controlling the anger. It said, "Save it. Save it for the game this afternoon."

How do you stop a friend from hurting himself? I'd been trying to decide what, if anything, I could do about Kevin. He had a date with a buyer third period. For all I knew, it could be the school narc. Why was he doing it? Wasn't it bad enough *he* was hooked without trying to involve others? And what could I do? He knew how I stood on the subject but he was as stubborn as Pete. As me, when it came to taking advice.

All through second period I couldn't concentrate. Between thinking about Laurel and imagining Kevin meeting some innocent freshman, maybe, maybe even the narc, and selling him dope, my mind was going around in circles. What should I do? What *could* I do?

And then I knew. He was to meet the buyer at his locker, at third period, probably where the stash must be. A surge of excitement rushed through me. Did I dare?

I knew his lock combination almost as well as my own, having stood by Kev's side a zillion times while he dialed. And I thought, when third period comes, if he doesn't have the stuff, he can't sell. Right? He'd wonder what happened. I could say . . . I could say—what? That I'd heard there was going to be a locker sweep? That I saved his hide by getting there before the narcs did? Would he buy that?

Or . . . I could just go in and take the stuff and dump it in the wastebin. And let him worry about what happened to it.

Either way, maybe it would put the fear of God into him. At least until he came to his senses.

And so, fifteen minutes before second period ended, I left American history and ran down the hall and up the stairs to Kevin's locker. Five minutes later I slammed it shut, holding a small plastic bag, which I jammed into my pocket. Going back down the stairs, feeling guilty as sin, who should I bump into but Mr. Wilson.

"Well, Cam, what are you doing out of class?" the principal asked.

"Er, just needed something in my locker," I stammered, sweating and fingering the bag in my pocket.

"So, we gonna win the league championship tonight?"

"Sure hope so, Mr. Wilson."

"We're all counting on you!"

"Yeah, I know, Mr. Wilson."

"Well, better get back to class, Potter," he said at last. "Good luck."

I skipped back down the stairs like I was carrying uranium, frantic to get rid of it as fast as I could. Two doors from the classroom, and without thinking through what it might mean to Kevin, I dropped the stuff into a trash can. Then, with a sigh of relief, I opened the door and returned to my seat just as Turner announced the next assignment.

Kevin found me as I headed for the gym to get my football gear, game adrenaline already flowing.

"Hey, Cam, wait up! I gotta talk to you!" He fell in step beside me. With nervous fingers he wiped the sweat off his brow. "You hear anything about a locker check?"

"I gotta go, Kev. Cooney goes crazy before a big game if we're a minute late." I hurried along the hall.

"I don't understand it!" He skipped ahead and faced me, walking backwards. "I had this little deal going down. Nothing big, you know? The stuff was in my locker. I brought it in this morning. This kid came by third period, and when I opened the locker—it was gone! You sure you didn't hear anything about a locker check?"

I shrugged, not saying yes or no. "What'll you do?"

Kevin scratched his head. "I don't know. Do you think someone could have seen me and stole the stuff? Nah. Who'd know the combination? And the lock wasn't broken, so . . . Geez. Could I be that far gone

that I left the stuff home and *thought* I brought it in?
Nah . . ."

We'd reached the gym lockers. Cooney wouldn't let
outsiders in, and Kevin, for all that he'd been on the
team for years, was now an outsider. I tapped my foot
nervously, knowing I should be inside, but I was respon-
sible for Kevin's worry, and he needed to talk.

"I could go home and check," Kevin said, looking
puzzled. "But I'm sure. Oh, man. Maybe it was security!" He drew a hand across his throat. "Oh, man! If it is
—am I in trouble!"

He seemed so jittery, I almost broke down and told
him the truth.

"I guess I'll just have to hang in there and hope!" he
cried. "If they're onto me, I'll hear, and soon! Man.
What a bummer! Why'd I ever take a dumb chance like
that?"

"Potter!" Cooney called, opening the door to the
gym and checking around. "Get in here." He nodded
distantly at Kevin then beckoned to me.

"Right, coach. In a sec." I turned back to Kevin. "Listen, Kev. I gotta go. You coming to the game tonight?"

"Yeah," he said without enthusiasm.

"See you later then. And hey—don't worry. It'll work
out okay."

The tension inside the locker room was what it's
probably like in a war room just before a major battle.
Guys silently gearing up, inside themselves. Or already
dressed and doing push-ups and stretch exercises. Or
nervously fiddling with anything to keep their hands
busy. Except for Warren and Bud, who were pounding

on each other's shoulder pads hard enough to knock each other out.

"Okay, you guys. Listen up!" Cooney said. "Thompson's gonna pass around some little extra something for each of you. And I want you all to take it. Now!"

I felt stretched as tight as a high wire and needed a "little extra something" like a heart attack. "What is it, coach?" I asked in a voice that didn't sound my own.

He stared me down. "I'm the coach around here. You either trust me, or get out." He swiveled his head slowly, making eye contact with each member of the team, then added, "All right. It's something new. Supposed to be the hottest—vitamin—on the market. Gonna give you that little extra zing so you can go out there and kill those guys!"

"I don't think I need it, coach," I mumbled, not expecting him to hear.

"You say something, Potter?" He cupped a hand around one ear. The whole team was watching.

"I don't think I need it."

"If I say you need it, then you need it," Cooney said. "Now, hop to it, all of you! The bus leaves for Santa Maria in ten minutes!"

Maybe there's something to coach psychology. If he makes his players mad enough at him, at the opposing team, at the world maybe, they'll spill it out on the playing field. Because that's the approach Cooney took before we went out to play.

"Listen up!" he said, standing with one foot on a low bench, hand on a hip, in the visitors' locker room. Little

Napoleon, Kevin had once called him, and the thought almost made me smile.

"This is the game that separates the men from the boys. This is it, guys," he bellowed. "This is the game you've busted your balls to get to. The league championship!" He paused to let the importance of it sink in, as if we didn't already know. "You're tough. You're mean. You know your stuff. You're gonna go out there and run right over them. Right?"

"Right!" we shouted on cue.

For a second I let myself wonder just how good Santa Maria really was. We'd never seen them play and this was our first encounter. Cooney talked them down to make us feel good, but from what I read about them in the papers, they didn't get to league finals by being wimps.

"Okay, you guys! Are you ready?"

"Yeah!"

"Are you gonna win?"

"Yeah!"

Cooney gave us a thumbs-up and a wide grin. "Then get out there and prove it!"

The pills must have worked, because as I led the way out to the field I felt the energy of a herd of bulls behind me. We were in shape, well coached, psyched to win. What more could we ask?

Those first minutes against an unknown opponent, you're kind of feeling them out, kind of appraising strengths and weaknesses. Those first minutes against Santa Maria I knew right away. They were *good*! They were tougher than us. Inside of three minutes we had to call time-out so Rollins, one of our tailbacks, could be carried off the field. They were meaner than us. I swear I saw one of their fullbacks foaming at the mouth. They were bigger. Next to them we looked like the girls' drill team.

No matter what Cooney said, we were in trouble.

They made the first touchdown by just steamrolling over us. Still fresh, we made the next touchdown by following game plan just as Cooney ordered. They made a second TD and then, by sheer force of will, and luck, so did we. But by half time it was 17 to 14, their favor. And we were losing some of our best players to injuries.

We trudged back to the lockers hurting, exhausted, scared of what Cooney would say. I'd seen him on the sidelines dancing a mad jig, sending wild hand signals, screaming words I couldn't hear.

"What's the matter with you guys?" Cooney shouted as soon as we all assembled. "You're playing like a bunch of girls. You're better than they are! You know that! How come you're letting them through?"

"They're tough, coach," I said, rubbing the calf of my right leg where three guys had sat on it. "We're trying."

"Don't tell me you're trying!" he screamed. "They're winning!"

"They're mowing us down, coach. We've lost some of our best guys."

"What are you talking about? Football's a contact sport. You expect injuries. Palmer? You okay?"

Palmer stared at the ground. Carbonetti had wrapped his leg with Ace bandages. "Sure, coach."

"Goldberg. You in too much pain to play?"

Goldberg, with an arm in a bucket of ice, glanced at me, grimaced, and said, "I've felt worse."

"Rollins?"

Rollins sat on a chair shivering. Carbonetti answered for him. "He's dislocated the right shoulder, Len."

"When I played football, I went out there with a cracked rib! We need him. Just put a harness on and give him a shot."

"Len, I don't know."

"Listen up, doc. I need him, understand? He can rest up all he wants—after the game."

"No," I said, surprising myself. Suddenly I saw Cooney the way Peter said he was—self-centered, out only for his own glory. If we won the league championship he'd be a hero to the school board, to the community. Maybe he could get a college coaching job. He'd do anything to win.

"Did you say no?" Cooney asked in disbelief.

"I don't mean to be disrespectful, sir, but we can manage without him." I surprised myself at how reasonable, how logical I sounded. "He's likely to favor the shoulder, so we won't get his best anyway, and those turds are mean. They'll spot his weakness and go after him just for spite. We'll manage. Griffin can sub."

"Griffin?"

"Yeah." I could almost see the wheels turning in Cooney's head as he visualized Griffin's skills.

"He's right, Len," Carbonetti agreed.

"All right!" Cooney said at last. "Rollins, you're out for the rest of the game. But I'm telling the rest of you, right now. This game means a lot to me. To us! To the school! You just better not screw up! You just better go out there and win!"

As I led the team back to the field fourth quarter my heart hammered so hard I thought it was coming loose. I'd decided to try something that could put me in real hot water, maybe get me off the team if it failed.

But the first plays were disaster city. The fullback I sent into the line came out holding his knee. He was carried off on a stretcher.

"Listen," I said during the time-out. "Cooney's gone off the deep end. We can win, but not his way. Those guys are too physical. We'll all wind up in the hospital if we follow his strategy. Maybe, if we use our heads, we've got a chance. I'm changing strategy."

"Hey, Cam. You can't! Cooney'll kill you!" Crunch said.

"You know what you're *doing*?"

"Noooo."

A couple of guys laughed nervously and I sensed an ease to the tension.

"You with me?"

"Yeah!"

We touched hands. I said a silent prayer, called the play, and we took positions.

With Cooney pacing on the sidelines like he'd like to come in and play the game for us, I put the first play into action. We were on the thirty-five yard line, fourth down, with nine yards to make for a first. I knew Santa Maria's strategy. As soon as I got the ball, I'd pull back to throw, but they'd hard-rush me, moving in like so many Sherman tanks, and there wouldn't be a hole to throw into. This time I let them come, but just before they reached me I dinked the ball over them to the blocking back, and while the tanks rolled over me, he took it to the twenty-five and we had a first down.

The second play they rushed me, just as before, but this time I used a screen pass and it worked like a charm. Our line let them penetrate like a hot knife going through butter, and hallelujah! Behind them was my wide receiver with four blockers in front of him, and while the tanks ran over me again, crushing my left leg, he ran it to the thirteen. And another first down.

The crowd went crazy. Cooney danced on the sidelines like he had a burr in his foot, punching the air with his fist again and again. I tried to disguise the pain as I limped back into the huddle.

"Hey, man! How 'bout that!" one of the guys exclaimed, as we touched hands.

"It ain't over yet!" I said. The adrenaline shot through me like water bursting from a dam and my mind went wild figuring what to do next. It worked twice, but would they be dumb enough to fall for it a third time? Probably not.

Well, what? I'd just play it by ear. Improvise.

"Sweep right," I barked. The guys looked puzzled, sensing the play couldn't work, but they followed instructions. "And this time, *block!*"

I limped forward, exaggerating my disability, and crouched behind the center, my right palm flat against his buttocks.

"Hut, hut!" I barked. "Hut, hut hut!"

The ball snapped into my hands. I pulled back and swung right to hand off to Griffin. I could see my guard pulling and double-teaming on the left corner of the defense. Just as I put the ball out for Griffin to enfold, I pulled back, swung around 180 degrees, and headed around the left end.

The team had followed the play design so well that Santa Maria's defense figured Griffin was carrying. And I was around the end and down to the five before a Santa Maria linebacker got an angle on me.

The leg hurt, damn it, hurt bad, but it had to wait. I launched my body for the flag. The linebacker crunched into me, and I flew over the goal line to the roar of the crowd screaming in my ears. I lay on the ground with the zebra standing over me, arms straight up like goalposts. I lay on the ground, hugging my leg, heart pounding, tears of pain running down my cheeks. And smiling.

We won. Not Cooney's way, but ours. Twenty-one to seventeen. How's that?

13

In the locker room it was Easter week and New Year's Eve rolled into one. We screamed and laughed and recounted every minute of the game, swigged beer and squirted it all over each other. I joked with Carbonetti as he packed ice on my swollen ankle, but watched the doorway, dreading the moment Cooney would appear. How would he take it?

The door opened and Cooney breezed in with two guys in tow. Right away you could tell that they thought Cooney was God's gift to the sports world. They hung on his every word. One of them had an arm around his shoulder. And Cooney beamed.

"Listen up, you guys!" he called out, taking his Little Napoleon stance, one foot up on the bench. "I'm proud of ya! You played one hell of a game! Every one of you!" He smiled around the room. "Isn't that right, Troy?" he asked of the man beside him.

"Absolutely! One hell of a game!"

"Real smart game," the second man said. "First rate team. Terrific coaching."

"Yea, coach!" someone yelled. "Hip hip hooray!"

One of our linebackers rushed forward and lifted

Cooney to his shoulders. He waltzed him around the room while guys sprayed Cooney with beer and he yelled to be put down.

Carbonetti packed up his stuff and moved away to work over another player as the two strangers approached me.

"How ya doing, Potter?" the heavyset guy with the beard who Cooney'd called Troy asked. "You were very good today. We were very impressed. Very."

"Yeah, thanks," I said. "We all played pretty well today."

The taller man took a card from his pocket and handed it to me. "Name's Larez. We've been watching you all season. You're looking better all the time. Put on some weight, too, haven't you?"

"Yeah," I admitted, warily. "About twenty pounds."

"Thought so. You'll need it—next year, in college."

"*If* I get to go. . . ."

"Oh, you'll go, all right. No doubt about that," Larez said. "Though you could use another twenty."

Another twenty pounds? "I'm working on it," I said, not looking the guy in the eye.

"So Cooney says. He's pretty high on you. Says you're a real winner. Get along swell with the guys. Stay out of trouble. Not into drugs." He smiled and put a hand on my shoulder. "Just the kind of athlete we like."

I smiled up at him, sweating, wondering if he could possibly tell by the zits, by the quick weight gain. Whether he knew and didn't care. "You *know* Cooney," I quipped. "If he says something, you better believe it."

"*Modest*, too," Troy said, laughing.

At which point Cooney joined us, wiping beer off his

face with a towel. "Don't trust these fellas, Cam. They're out to get you cheap." He gave me a knowing wink, but there was no humor in it. If he didn't like my changing game plan, I sure wasn't going to find out about it now. "So," he said, punching me on the shoulder, "shall we all go out and celebrate?"

I got home around midnight, done in from the game and all the beer afterwards. My ankle throbbed, but it wasn't broken, only twisted. All I wanted to do was sack out.

"That you, Cam?" Dad called from the kitchen. "Come on in. Have some coffee with me."

He came out of the kitchen to meet me in the hall, all smiles. "That was one swell game, I tell you! I was so proud I nearly busted a gut!"

I limped after him into the kitchen and yawned. "Man, I'm bushed."

"Bet you are! Here. Mom specially baked your favorite cookies, chocolate chip, and don't tell me they're not on your diet. Just sit down and enjoy!"

I took a quart of milk from the fridge and poured a tall glass, then went to the table.

"So tell me! What happened afterwards? What did Cooney say? What about those scouts? You know, I read they're under a lot of pressure to win. The alumni, the administration—they're on their backs all the time. If they lose three, four seasons in a row they're *out!*"

I eyed the cookies greedily, then took a couple.

"Those coaches talk to you? Mom and I sat right in front of them at the game. You should have heard what they said about Cooney!"

"What did they say about Cooney?" I asked, ignoring my conscience and popping a cookie in my mouth. It was still warm, with the chocolate soft and oozie and loads of nuts. I closed my eyes and purred, "Umm . . . Mom sure knows how to make these."

"Well," Dad said, leaning across the table toward me, "I was so busy watching the game and yelling your name that I didn't even listen, until your mother nudged me." He paused, waiting for me to look interested.

"So, what did you hear?" I asked, stuffing another cookie into my mouth.

"This guy with the beard snickered at the way Cooney was acting. You know how crazy he gets. He said if it weren't for Cooney's record of turning out first-rate athletes, they'd never even give him the time of day."

I smiled, remembering how Troy had fawned all over coach. "Did they say anything about me?"

"Sure did! When you took over in the last quarter they were practically drooling! Especially when you faked out the whole team and got that touchdown! That tall guy said—and don't quote me, now, but it was something like—" Dad dropped his voice to sound like Larez— " 'That Potter's good! Got a head on his shoulders. Watch Cooney. He doesn't know whether to cheer or blow a fuse. Bet ya Potter didn't follow Cooney's game plan!' You didn't, right?"

"Right." I refilled the milk glass.

Dad's eyes watered, and his voice grew husky. "You did what I never could when I was in college, Cam, what your brother never could. I'm real proud of you."

I thought of spoiling Dad's pleasure by saying, "Would you be proud if you knew I was taking steroids, something Pete would never do?" But I didn't. Instead I said "Thanks, pops" and changed the subject. "You talk to Pete lately?"

Dad's smile faded. "Don't talk to me about your brother."

"Don't you want to know what he's doing? Did you know he's signed up two jobs for the guys already? Did you know he's trying to cut down on smoking? Did you know . . ."

Dad cut me off with a wave of his hand. "He quit when I needed him; that's all that counts with me. He's a quitter. You watch. When the going gets rough, he'll find some excuse to bail out on those friends of his. Pete's like that. Don't you know? He's never gonna make it like you."

"Aw, Dad!" I cried in disgust. "You always put him down! You know it was no picnic working for you. He had guts hanging in there as long as he did. So he left! So what? He's trying to make it on his own! Doesn't that count for something?"

Dad scratched his beard and gazed into the corner of the room. "Pete's too much like me!" he said softly. "Maybe he *looks* like your mother, but *you're* the one like her. She's the one with sticking power. She's the one kept me from giving up whenever things got too rough. Now, Pete . . ."

"Dad . . ." I started, not really knowing what to say. Lamely I added, "Business will improve. It always has." I reached across the table to touch him. "You're okay in my book."

Dad shrugged and didn't answer. Slowly he dragged himself up from the chair. "It's late. I'm sorry. I've kept you up much too long."

I rose and put the near-empty milk carton back in the fridge. "Dad?"

"What?" he asked, wrapping his robe tighter around his legs. His eyes were bloodshot and there were fine lines around the corners I'd never noticed before.

"I just want you to know. Pete loves you. . . . And so do I."

The first thing I thought when I awoke the next morning was that I should never have drunk all that beer. My head felt like it had been invaded by a rock band. My ankle throbbed, even without weight being put on it. I postponed facing the world and thought about Kevin. Had he come to the game? I'd phone him. Maybe he'd want to drive up to Santa Barbara with me to visit Pete today. The two-hour drive would be a good place to talk.

The second thing I thought about was Laurel. I just couldn't believe she didn't feel the same as I did, that she wasn't as turned on by me as I by her. There had been so many clues: the night of the dance, the way she fit so perfectly against my body; the reaction to me when she jumped off the swing into my arms. How could she turn away from feelings like that? I mean—so I behaved like a caveman for a minute. Okay, I was ashamed. But couldn't she forgive?

The third thing I thought about was Mike. I'd heard at the gym that he'd been released from the hospital.

And here it was two weeks and I still hadn't called his home. How come I kept putting it off?

Gingerly I climbed out of bed and pulled on my jeans, washed up, and took one of the pain killers. Then went in for breakfast.

"Must have been some party," Mom said, bringing the milk container and a glass to the table. "Bacon and eggs?"

"Just coffee." I took a cup from the cabinet and brought the coffeepot to the table, hoping Mom would understand and not want to blister the air with talk about last night's game. Her eyes widened and she kept quiet, for which I silently thanked her.

Somewhere I'd read that after you've been taking steroids awhile the first feelings of exhilaration disappear and you feel sluggish. That's how I felt, like it would take a derrick to get me up. I didn't know if it was a reaction to the game and the drinking, or to the pile-up of steroids, or to a combination of them all. I needed caffeine, lots of it, and maybe even some uppers, to face the day. Did we have any? And then I thought, "Jeez, what's this? A month ago I wouldn't put *anything* chemical into my body and now I'm looking for uppers and if the uppers make me too hyper, I'll need a downer." I closed my eyes and sipped more coffee.

"I thought I'd visit Pete today," I said after a while. "Want to come?"

Head cocked, Mom studied me, a worried expression on her face. "I don't know, Cam," she said, not answering my question. "That diet you're on can't be all that good if it makes your skin break out like that. Maybe you should see a dermatologist."

"Jeez!" I cried, leaping up to my feet, stressing the ankle. "Let me alone! There's nothing wrong with me! I don't need a dermatologist, or any other kind of doctor! I'm just fine!"

"Cam . . . Cam . . ." Mom protested as I pushed my chair back and glared at her. "What's wrong? You're so touchy lately! All I said was . . ."

"Just leave me alone!" I shouted, shoving my chair into the table. "I'm not a baby anymore! I know what I'm doing! Just leave me alone!"

Mom didn't deserve my tirade. I knew that as I left the room. But I couldn't do as she asked, see a doctor. What if he ran blood tests? How would that sit with the scouts if it got out? Sure, plenty of college athletes took steroids, and other stuff, too, but as long as it wasn't public knowledge, no one complained. Anyway, what harm was I doing by taking the dianabol? So what if it gave me a little acne. And maybe made me a bit aggressive. And . . .

Well, it wouldn't last forever. And the payoff was worth it—a college scholarship to a top school. That's what Troy and Larez offered.

And all I needed was another twenty pounds.

14

The way I felt, I wanted to get out of the house as fast as possible, so I phoned Kevin about going to Santa Barbara and we arranged to meet at eleven. Then, feeling uneasy without reason, I dialed Mike's house, but as the phone rang, so did our doorbell. I could hear Mom greeting someone who sounded suspiciously like Amy.

I hung up and went to the door, curious and surprised. Amy had never come to the house before. What could she want?

Standing in the doorway with the light behind her she gave me a moment's pang. She looked so fresh and pretty, like a spring flower, with her hair tied back in a blue ribbon and a yellow and white sweater over white jeans. Her face brightened as soon as she saw me. Nervously pushing her hair back, she poured out a torrent of words. "Could you come out for a while? Take a walk? I should have called, I know, but . . . I need to ask you something."

"If it's not too far." I nodded at my foot. "And not too long. I'm leaving for Santa Barbara in an hour."

"Oh. Okay. I've got the car."

* * *

As she drove, she talked excitedly about the game with Santa Maria and how she and the pep squad had nearly gone crazy that last quarter. "You were absolutely sensational!" she exclaimed, taking my hand. I moved closer and put an arm around her, pleasantly aware of her perfume, a musky, exotic scent she usually wore when we dated.

"What do you say we drive to the Meadows?" I said, thinking how nice it would be to get out and walk on one of the many trails leading from the meadow to some private place. I wanted to take Amy in my arms and forget about Laurel. This was the girl I should be caring for. She appreciated the same things I did; we never argued. She enjoyed making out just as I did—at least until Laurel came into the picture.

"The Meadows it is," she said, as I leaned over and kissed her quickly.

Hand in hand we walked up one of the trails and stopped where no one would see us if they passed. Amy leaned against a rock. And we kissed. And kissed some more. I felt her face grow warm against my cheek. She made little pleasure sounds as she slid her hands under my shirt and caressed my back.

And I—felt nothing. I knew everything that was happening. I smelled her exciting perfume, and liked the touch of her hands and the soft, then increasingly passionate, kisses.

But.

I felt nothing.

I shivered. What was the matter with me? Couldn't anyone turn me on except Laurel now? Was it the steroids? Why?

Abruptly, I drew back, holding her around the waist, not able to look her in the eyes.

"What's wrong?" she asked in a low voice.

"Nothing."

"There is! I can tell! Don't you like me anymore?"

"Sure I like you! I always have! It's not that. I'm just—not in the mood." I pushed her hair out of one eye. "So tell me. What was it you wanted to talk to me about?"

She shuddered suddenly, as if cold, and I put my arms around her. Her heart beat like a frightened bird against me and I hated myself for being aware of it.

"I thought . . ." she said into my chest, "I thought . . . a couple of the girls are wearing their boyfriends' varsity jackets. I thought . . ." She stopped. "Oh, I can't say it. It's really something you ought to think of yourself!"

"You want to wear my varsity jacket?" I smiled at her upraised face. If anyone deserved to wear it, Amy did. "Sure. Why not? Here." I pulled away and took off the jacket. Her face lit up with pleasure as I helped her into it. Giving her the jacket seemed some kind of compensation for something. I didn't quite know what.

"Let's go," I said, taking her hand. "I hate to leave but I promised Kevin I'd pick him up by eleven. I'll call you when I get back."

"So what'd you do after the game?" Kevin asked as we settled into the car. He slumped in the seat beside me and crossed his arms over his chest, preparing to sleep.

"The usual. Lots of dissecting every play. Lots of beer. Lots of horsing around. The usual."

We were driving south to the freeway. Joggers chugged along the shoulder of the road, Walkmans attached to their ears. The sky was clear and blue and the wind ruffled the palm fronds high up on the tree stems. A great day.

"I miss the guys. I hate to admit it, but I even miss Cooney and the fun we had after a win," Kevin said. "But last night I was too bummed out over where that pot stash went to care. I still can't figure it!"

A surge of guilt rushed through me as I considered whether to tell Kevin not to worry. He looked as if he hadn't slept a whole lot last night, and in his place I wouldn't have either.

"The way I figure, someone had to have got my locker combination and taken the stuff, otherwise I'd have heard, don't you think?"

I made a sound halfway between yes and no.

"Well, don't you?"

"Yeah, I guess so," I said.

"Then all I'm out is some dough. All I gotta do is change the combination and I'm back in business." Kevin sat straighter, satisfied with his own analysis.

I took my eyes off the road to peer at him. "You're kidding! I thought you said it wasn't worth the risk!"

He smiled. "Only if you're caught, my man. Only if you're caught."

"Jeez, Kev!" I cried, checking the rearview mirror before taking a right onto the 134. "It's one thing smoking a joint now and then for fun. That's your business. But you're talking about dealing and that's illegal!"

"And what you're doing isn't?"

"There's nothing illegal about taking steroids!"

"Without a doctor's prescription?"

"Mike probably has a doctor's prescription."

"Whose? Carbonetti's?" He laughed in disbelief. "And for whom? You?"

"Aw, shut up. It's not the same. And you know it!"

"Yeah? Where do you think the stuff comes from? Not from American drug houses, you can bet on that. Not without a prescription."

"So it comes from Mexico. So what? Where do you think your *weed* comes from? You think that's so pure?"

Kevin smirked. "I like to play Russian roulette. Sue me. I just didn't know you did too. Besides, what I smoke doesn't stop *me* from 'getting it up.' What about you?"

"Shit!" I exploded as my face began to burn. "You don't know the first thing about it!"

"If you say so. Just lay off bugging *me* about my thing and I'll lay off *you* about yours."

Kevin closed his eyes and went to sleep, head against the window, while I drove in angry silence. Kevin would keep on smoking pot because he depended on it just as much as he used to depend on drink. He'd go on dealing and for sure get caught eventually. And me? To win that scholarship I needed twenty more pounds, so I'd keep on taking the pills like Mike said, regardless of the side effects, regardless of the ethics or legality. Life sure wasn't simple.

Kevin woke up a few miles south of Santa Barbara, when I left the freeway. He read out the directions to the house Pete was living in and we climbed higher and higher into the hills.

"Luck-y!" Kevin whistled as I pulled off the road into the driveway. Pete's van was in the garage. Two surfboards leaned against one wall and a racing bike hung from a roof rafter. Most of the garage was taken up with shovels and rakes, wheelbarrows and cement mixers, sacks of cement mix and stacks of ten-foot plastic pipe.

We climbed out of the car, stretched, and went to the edge of the cliff. "Wow!" I exclaimed. Below, a hundred-and-eighty-degree view of the ocean sparkled blindingly in the noon sun. I could almost feel the worry and anger melting away.

"Hey, man! You made it!" Pete called, bounding out of the house in cutoffs and a T-shirt. "Heaven is never having to leave the beach," the shirt read.

"You thought maybe we'd get lost?" I teased, throwing my arms around him. "Hey, big brother! You've lost weight! You're positively skinny!" I drew back to look at him.

"Ten pounds," Pete announced, puffing his chest out. "You put it on and I take it off. Pretty good arrangement, huh?" He beckoned to us. "Come on in and see the place. We've really got a deal. Some rich widow bought the house, then decided to go to Spain. Jason pays a paltry rent in exchange for taking care of the grounds. Come meet the guys."

The bearlike hairy one was Jason, Pete said, the landscape architect with a degree in botany. Short and wiry Tom was the cement contractor and a genius, according to Pete, in building waterfalls.

"So this is the kid brother," Jason said when we entered the kitchen. He turned from the sink, where he was washing apples, and extended a wet hand for me to shake. Tom nodded a welcome and set a platter of cheese and fruit on a table looking out to a flower-bordered lawn.

"All this health food! I thought you were a fast-food freak," I told Pete, helping myself to some jack cheese.

"The operative word is 'was,' " Jason called out. "He's seen the light."

"And no smokes? My, my. I barely recognize you without the smell of nicotine."

Pete threw up his hands and his lips twisted into an embarrassed grin. "What can I say? These guys are freaks, I'm telling you. No booze, except for a little vino now and then. No pot. No cigarettes in the house"—he pulled a pack from his pocket and waved it at me—"not to say I've given them up completely."

We settled at the table and caught up on news about school and football and life in Santa Barbara but stayed off the personal. I wanted time alone with Pete to do that. They joked about each other's idiosyncrasies and talked hopefully about future jobs coming in because "We're good. We're neat. We're dependable, and last but not least, we're . . . cheap." We spent part of the afternoon shmoozing like that, munching on apples and pears, shelling nuts, finishing off the cheeses and crackers. And finally, when the table was cleared, Jason and Tom took off to finish a job. Kevin sacked out on the couch. And Pete and I went off for a walk on the beach.

"Remember when we did this last?" Pete asked as we shed our shoes and walked along the near-deserted shore. Gulls squawked overhead, occasionally diving down to snatch something from the sea. The briny scent was strong, bringing back memories.

"Oregon? That vacation when we drove to Seattle? When was it? I was around eight, I think. Remember the bottles of sand crabs we collected?"

Pete chuckled. "Yeah. I think you figured Dad would cook them for dinner."

I punched him lightly on the arm. "I did not!"

"So how is the old man?" Pete asked. We walked along kicking up sand, picking up an occasional rock and skimming it out across the water.

"Missing you. He won't admit it, but he does. He needs you, Pete. He took your leaving hard. He can't like himself if you don't like him."

"Oh, sure," Pete said, without conviction.

"Why don't you forget pride and phone him?"

"Look. I can't. He gets under my skin. He makes me want to do anything to get his goat."

"You don't have to go home. All I'm saying is—call him sometime."

"I'll think about it," Pete said. "Now, how about you?"

I told him about my last encounters with Laurel and how I didn't know what more I could say or do to get her back, apart from begging. "Besides," I started, and then stopped.

"Besides?" Pete repeated.

I shrugged. "I don't know if it's the steroid, or what, but I seem to be . . . er . . . having . . . trouble . . . in the sex department."

"You mean impotence?"

I nodded, beginning to sweat at having to admit

something so personal. "I thought maybe it's because I've been under so much pressure, you know. It's kind of the last thing on my mind right now."

"At your age? Come on! Don't kid yourself. Go off the dianabol."

"How can I? These guys, scouts, were at the last game. They want me to put on another twenty pounds! I've been eating like an elephant. Exercising religiously. Taking the pills, even increasing the dose . . . and I've only gained twenty-two pounds so far."

"Increasing the dose? On your own? You crazy?"

"Listen. Cut it out. Kevin read me the riot act on the drive up. Another month and I can stop. Maybe."

"Damn it, Cam! What if the folks knew?"

"You tell them and I swear, I'll never talk to you again!"

Pete opened his mouth and shut it. He picked up a cola can weighted with sand and threw it with all the force he had.

"Damned if I'd take a chance on some chemical messing up my body! You don't need to be a bruiser! Screw those guys!"

"Listen, Pete. I want that scholarship. Laurel made me realize I don't want to be only a 'jock' for the rest of my life. Anyway, stop worrying. How dangerous can it be if lots of college athletes take it?"

"Where'd you get your statistics? From Cooney? Sure, he'd tell you others do it so you'll feel safe. Plenty of college players don't take anything. They just work hard and count on their natural ability!"

"Can it, Pete. I'm sick of the lectures! I'll do what I have to. Now lay off!"

"Oh, damn," Pete exclaimed. "Damn, damn, damn." He slammed his fist into his hand. "Okay. If that's what you want. But I wish you'd . . ."

"Race you to the pier," I said, cutting him off.

15

Monday morning I really felt down. The ankle hurt more than at first. The visit to Pete rankled because I knew he wasn't all wrong. Kevin's attitude about dealing nagged at me and I couldn't see how I could help. The impulsive gift I'd given Amy seemed a terrible mistake. She'd take it to mean more than I intended.

I eased out of bed and went to the bathroom to weigh myself. Up a pound over the weekend. Fifteen to go.

Pete had teased that I'd turn into a freak with all that weight and muscle, but because of the conscientious workouts, my body looked solid and powerful.

The skin, now, was another story. I reached for the medicated blemish cream that the guys said they used and smeared it on the latest eruption. And then, with a sigh, I unscrewed the pill bottle and poured the morning chemicals into my palm. Besides the three super vitamins, I now took ten dianabol capsules before breakfast, lunch, dinner, and bedtime, a total of two hundred fifty milligrams a day. Too much? Mike said at one time he'd been taking five hundred. I tilted my head back and tossed the pills in my mouth, considering upping the dose. Maybe I could gain the necessary weight faster and then give it up.

But could I keep the weight on if I stopped?

I dragged myself in to breakfast, set out the prescribed calories, protein, and carbohydrates, and, leaning my head on the palm of my left hand, shoveled it in. And then, with the enthusiasm of a slug, went off to school.

Amy must have been watching for me, because as soon as I reached the quad she separated herself from her friends and appeared at my side.

"Hi, darling!" she said, reaching up to kiss me and speaking loud enough for others to hear. I thought, *Hey, wait a minute!* She wore my red and gold varsity jacket, which hung loosely on her slender frame. Linking arms, she asked, "How's the ankle?"

"Better." I shifted books to free my arm.

"Guess what? Crunch and Sue just announced they're going steady! And they only met for the first time at my party! Would you believe? He gave her his class ring!"

Well, don't expect that from me, I said silently as she maneuvered me toward our friends.

"Show it to Cam!" Amy exclaimed as we joined the circle.

"Amy! I *know* what a class ring looks like!" I said, glancing around anxiously. The whole scene made me very uncomfortable. I didn't like the pressure Amy was applying. And I didn't want to hurt her by spelling out that wearing my jacket didn't mean we'd be going steady.

"Look! I gotta go in!" I said abruptly. "See you later, guys . . . Amy." I disentangled myself and hurried off.

"Hey, Cam! Wait!" she called, running after me. "What's the hurry? It's still ten minutes before the bell!"

I saw Laurel approaching, walking with friends. Exasperated, I said, "Look. I'll see you later, okay?"

"Sure." The bright smile faded. "You're not angry with me, are you?"

"Of course not!" I looked over Amy's shoulder and caught Laurel's eye. My face grew warm.

"Well, *okay*, then!" Amy said, satisfied. She stuck her hands deep into the pockets of my jacket, stood on tiptoe, and gave me a quick kiss. Just as Laurel passed.

"Hi," I said, waylaying Laurel on her way to first-period English. Worried that she might tell me to get lost, I smiled tentatively and fell in step beside her. "When are you going to give me my next tennis lesson?"

She kept on walking, not answering me.

"You can't be that hard-hearted," I said. "I'm not asking you to marry me, just to teach me the game."

She glanced at my leg. "You don't look like you'll be up to that kind of thing for a while."

I cocked my head and said, "You don't know my magic healing powers. How about Saturday?"

"I already told you, Cam. It won't work. We're too different."

"Opposites attract."

"Fire and water don't mix."

"But put them together and you'll sure get a lot of steam!"

"Hot air, you mean."

I laughed and threw up my hands. "You win. So how about it? Just tennis. I won't hassle you for anything more."

We'd arrived at the door to the English class. Amy was waiting. Watching. Which didn't escape Laurel. It may even have counted in my favor, either easing her suspicion about my motives or making her a mite envious.

"Hi, Laurel," Amy said, pairing off at my side.

Laurel searched my face, then Amy's. "All right," she said. "Ten o'clock. Same place. And don't be late!" She swept by us and went into the classroom.

I sat through English with a grin bubbling inside me. Hope. That's what made the difference. Taking tennis lessons from Laurel was a foot in the door. I'd have a chance to reconnect, and if I went slowly, maybe we could start seeing each other again. I felt like leaping to my feet, jumping up and down, and crying "Yeouw!" But what would she say if she found out I'd lied about the steroids?

"He can see you for a short visit," Mike's wife said on the phone. "He tires easily."

I bought a small bouquet of flowers at the local market, some purple and white things that looked fresher than the daisies. Feeling foolish, and more than a little apprehensive, I arrived at Mike's house around four.

It was a small tract home on a dead-end street, busy with kids playing ball on the road. A tricycle lay overturned on the front lawn. I never knew Mike had a kid.

"He's inside," his wife said when she opened the door. A pretty, trim woman wearing gray sweats, she led me through an untidy living room to a hall. "Sorry for the mess. I haven't had time to pick up since I got home," she said. A little kid who looked like Mike toddled after her, finger in his mouth. She picked him up and led the way to a back bedroom.

"Honey? You've got a visitor!" she called, opening the door.

Mike sat in a bathrobe on a chair near a window, a book open on his lap. His skin color was funny, kind of pasty-yellow, and he seemed to have lost a good deal of weight since I saw him last.

"Hi!" I said, feeling awkward. "I brought these." I thrust the flowers out to Mike, who thanked me and passed them on to his wife.

"So, Mike! How ya doing?"

"Great! Hey. Good to see you! Sit down. Bring that chair over. Di? This is Cam Potter. Cam, my wife Diane."

"Hi," I said, moving the chair close to Mike.

She nodded and left the room to get a vase for the flowers, leaving me with Mike.

"So . . . how's it going?" I asked again. "When you coming back to the gym? The guys said you had a bad time."

Mike nodded. "Real bad. But let's not talk about me. I hear you did a job on the Santa Maria team! I hear the scouts are standing in line with offers. Didn't I tell you they would?"

"Oh, yeah, sure," I said, chuckling. "They're watching, all right, but no offers yet."

We talked about the plays in the last game and Mike listened intently. Finally he said, "You look good, Cam. How much weight you put on?"

"Twenty-two pounds. But I'm aiming for another eighteen."

"Yeah," Mike said. "That would be good." He looked away, and for the first time since I'd entered the room there was an awkward silence.

"Here. I brought you some tea and cookies," Diane said, carrying in a snack tray on which she'd put two cups and a plate of Oreo cookies. "You take sugar, Cam?"

"Not in front of Mike," I said, making him laugh.

Diane lifted the book from Mike's lap and handed him a steaming cup of tea. As she tossed the book on the bed I got a quick glimpse at the title. An electric charge went through me as I caught one word—*cancer.*

I sipped my tea and tried not to stare at Mike, but my head teemed with questions. Was he sicker than we'd been told? Is that why intensive care wouldn't give out info? Is that why it was taking so long for him to come back to work?

"How you doing with the steroid?" Mike asked, once his wife left the room.

"How do you mean? Side effects?" I wondered if I dared come right out, point blank, and ask if he had cancer. "Yeah, Mike. I've had a few." I touched the spots on my face. "Zits. That's one problem. And I'm not the sweet, good-natured guy I used to be, friends say. In addition . . ." I was just about to tell him about the low sex drive when he interrupted.

"How much you taking? A hundred a day, like I told you?"

"Two fifty."

His fingers tightened around the cup. "Two fifty? Who told you to take that much?"

"Nobody. I did it on my own. It's taking forever to put on that weight, Mike. I haven't got much more time. It's no cinch; you told me so yourself!"

"You monitoring your blood pressure?" Mike put his cup down. *"Are* you?"

"No. Should I? What's the big fuss? You've been on five hundred."

"Yeah. That's right! And man, am I paying the devil his due now!"

I stared at Mike. His lips trembled. I looked the other way while he blew his nose. He seemed to be trying to hide his face behind the tissues.

"It wasn't my appendix," he said at last. "They thought so at first. But it wasn't. It's my liver. I've got cancer."

"Oh, *man!*" I cried.

"Yeah," he said.

I didn't know what to say, or how to comfort him. Should I ask if he'd get better? What if he said it was terminal?

"Doctors say it's the steroids I've been on." He stared hard at me, willing me to contradict the doctors. "Just bad luck. That's all. Lots of guys take the stuff and nothing happens. Just the luck of the draw."

I got a scared lump in the pit of my stomach and the palms of my hands turned sweaty. "Maybe I should cut down?"

"Maybe. I've been thinking about that. But you're so close to your goal! Your whole future depends on giving those scouts what they want." He paused, lifted a cookie from the plate, examined it with distaste, and put it back. "Listen. Don't you be scared off by what's happening to me. I'll lick this thing, believe me. I'm not going to take this lying down. I'm a fighter! You know that!" Tough, stoic Mike started to cry suddenly, big, gasping sobs. Embarrassed for him, I turned away, then ran out to the hall and called Diane. I watched from the doorway while she helped Mike into bed, cooing encouragement, assuring him that he was only very tired and he'd be fine after he'd had a rest.

The baby toddled down the hall, screaming for his mother. I picked him up, patted him awkwardly, and promised Diane would be right there. But I was little comfort, because he strained against my hold, reaching his arms out toward Mike's room.

When Diane finally appeared and took the child from me her face seemed pinched, older than when I'd first come into the house.

As we said good-bye at the door she said, "He's scared of the chemotherapy, you see. It starts tomorrow."

16

I had a lot to think about.

For a while I just drove around aimlessly, reliving the visit with Mike, rehearing his sobs, reseeing Diane's wide-eyed fear, refeeling the kid's insecurity. And then I drove to the high school and parked. It was dark already, but the football field floods were on. I jogged to the fence and scaled it. And then I ran, eyes on the ground in front of me, mind blank. Ran until my ankle throbbed, until my leg ached. Ran until my breath escaped in gasps. Until I bent over double and threw up.

"You're late!" Dad called from the dinner table as I hurried by to shower and change. "We were worried. Ever hear of Ma Bell?"

"Not now," I mumbled under my breath.

"Where were you?" Mom asked when I came to the table. "Help yourself to salad. I'll go reheat your dinner."

Dad's hands circled his coffee cup while he watched me over the rim. "You okay, Cam? Something wrong?"

I nodded. "Mike, the guy who owns the gym? He's got liver cancer."

"Oh; I'm sorry to hear that."

"Yeah. Me too. He's not even thirty. And he's got a kid yet."

"That *is* sad. How long does he have?"

"What do you mean—*how long*? They're treating him. He'll get better!"

Dad put his cup down. "Not from what I hear. Cancer of the liver is usually fatal. Anyway, why are you taking it so hard? It's sad, sure, but you hardly know him and you aren't particularly fond of him, either."

I stared at Dad and then down at my plate. "He was taking steroids."

I could see Dad absorbing that fact. "*You* aren't on them, are you?"

My pulse raced as I glared at Dad. For all the promises I'd made about keeping the dianabol secret from Mom and Dad, here it was—the moment of truth. Should I tell, or not? "Why do you ask?"

"It's obvious. *Are* you?"

Some obstinate streak surfaced and without weighing the consequences I said, "As a matter of fact, I am."

Dad's eyes widened and he half rose from his chair, then dropped back again.

Mom returned from the kitchen with a plate loaded with food. "Here." She placed it before me. "The beef's not going to taste as good as it did an hour ago, but I can't help that."

"What?" Dad asked as if he could barely control his anger. "What are you taking?"

"Dianabol. It's like testosterone."

"Why? You're good enough without going that route!"

"Meaning, if I *wasn't* good enough it *would* be okay?"

"Meaning you shouldn't take it at all!"

"Look, Dad, it's very simple. Those scouts have all spelled it out. It's—put on thirty to forty pounds, or someone else gets picked." I speared a hunk of beef and viciously cut into it.

"What are you two talking about?" Mom asked.

"Did Pete put you up to this?"

"For Christ's sake, pops!" I cried. "He's been after me to quit!"

"Well! I never thought I'd be saying this, but he's smarter than you are!"

"For heaven's sake, what's going on here?" Mom asked, looking from me to Dad and back again. Dad held up a hand to hold her off while he glared at me. I played with the mashed potatoes, not looking at either of them.

"I'm going to talk to Cooney!" Dad announced.

I cried, "Oh no, you're not!"

"Oh yeah? Give me one good reason why!"

"Because he already knows. Who do you think sent me to Mike?"

That stopped him, but for only a moment. "All right. I'll go to the principal then!" He turned to Mom. "Would you believe? We entrust our kids to the schools and behind our backs they encourage drug use!"

"What?" Mom asked. "What are you talking about?"

I pushed my plate away while Dad explained what it was all about to Mom. "Stop it!" I bellowed, jumping up. "I'm seventeen years old! I'm not a kid anymore. It's my body and my life. Now stay out of it!"

"Cam . . ." Mom pleaded.

"Mom!"

"We're still your parents!"

"You want me to win that scholarship?"

"Of course!" Dad said. "But not at the risk of your health!"

"Nothing will happen to me! Darn! I'm sorry I told you. Now—leave—me—alone!"

I was flipping Larez's business card with the nail of one finger and wondering if I dared call him, when the phone rang and it was Amy. "Tell her I'm not in!" I hissed when Mom came to my room.

"You tell her!" Mom said, arms crossed over her bosom. "And while you're at it, tell her what you're doing to yourself. See what *she* says about that!"

I pushed by Mom to take the phone in the hall, angry at Amy for pestering me.

"Hi," I said without a shred of warmth. "What's up, Amy?"

"Is something wrong?" She read my voice correctly. "Is this a bad time to call?"

"Not the greatest. What did you want?"

"I just wondered if you could come over this evening," she said, coyly. "You know. We could talk. And stuff . . ."

She couldn't have chosen worse timing. I thought for a moment about going to Amy's and telling her about Mike and everything. Maybe she could help me sort it all out. But immediately I decided against it. Amy was a good-time girl. She wanted what she thought I was—a strong, decisive winner. Anything less would confuse her.

"No," I said. "I'm not going out."

"*Not* because you can't, or *not* because you don't want to," she asked, sounding a mite snippy.

"I don't want to."

"Oh." I could just see Amy's pretty blue eyes harden. "I thought we were going steady."

What a bastard I was becoming. Sure, she'd have assumed that. But still I asked, "Where'd you get that idea?"

"From you! You gave me your varsity jacket! I told everyone!"

"Amy," I said, exasperated with myself for not having been clear with her in the beginning, and with her for clinging to me like a stubborn sheet of cellophane wrap. I stopped myself from saying the first thing that came to mind, that *she'd* asked to wear the jacket; I hadn't offered. Instead I said, "Amy, listen. I like you. I like you a lot, but the jacket doesn't mean we're going steady. Understand?"

"Oh!" Amy cried. "Oh! . . . You'll want the jacket back!"

"No. Oh, no! Of course not! Amy, Amy, don't cry! Amy, please don't!" I said, wondering how I'd gotten into such a mess. "Just keep the jacket. Okay? It doesn't matter! And, Amy? Don't worry. We'll still see a lot of each other."

When we hung up I let out a deep breath. For all that the guys thought I was a real lady's man, I sure didn't know the first thing about women.

*   *   *

And then I pulled out Larez's business card and without allowing myself too long to think, dialed his number.

"Yes, Cam, of course I remember you," Larez's deep voice said. My hands sweated as I grasped the phone tighter. "What can I do for you?"

"Well, er . . . I just wanted to know . . . er . . . how serious you were about me as a player. I mean . . ." I rushed to add, so I wouldn't sound too eager, "there are other guys interested, and I would like to go with you, but . . ."

"Very. We're very interested," Larez said. "Providing, of course, that you put on a bit more muscle and bulk. You know. We told you when we were at your last game."

"You mean you wouldn't want me unless I put on another twenty pounds?"

Larez hesitated and then said, "I didn't say that."

Yes you did, I wanted to say. Instead I left a silence for him to elaborate.

"You're a darn good quarterback, Cam," Larez went on, oiling the waters. "You *think* on your feet; that's a valuable asset. Not all quarterbacks do."

Enough sweet talk, I thought. Answer my question.

"I don't say that you wouldn't be useful just as you are," Larez continued. "But I have to consider that you're likely to suffer greater injuries if you're not as heavy as we think you should be."

"With less weight I could be faster," I said.

"True. Yes. Be that as it may."

"So what's the bottom line?" I held my breath.

"I really can't say, Cam. We'd like you to be heavier; I already said that. We'll just have to add up the pros and cons when we've seen all the possibilities."

"Right."

"We do look forward to having you with us next year, Cam. *If* things work out for all concerned."

Thanks a bunch, I thought.

"Please let us know if you have any other questions."

In the end, the decision was mine to make. Not Cooney's or Mike's, not Pete's or Kevin's, not Mom's or Dad's. Just mine.

So where do you stand, sweetheart? I asked myself when I replaced the receiver. *You gonna go along with the pros and give them what they want? Or you gonna do it your way—at the risk of losing what you want? Time to piss or get off the pot . . . as the saying goes.*

It's not so easy to decide, my wimpy side argued. *If I quit the pills now, by next month when State comes by to make offers, or when Larez and his pals are ready to decide, I could have lost a good part of what I put on. I could look puny compared to the rest of the talent out there.*

I could also have a stroke, break somebody's neck on the playing field, wind up with liver problems, get shriveled-up balls. Among other things.

What would Laurel say?

Oh, shut up!

Stop asking yourself what so-and-so would say or think. What do *you* think?

If nothing ever developed between Laurel and me,

at least one good thing came out of knowing her. She made me realize that I wanted to be valued for more than just being a "hunk."

That day I threw away the dianabol capsules. I stayed on the diet and exercise regime and kept up the high potency vitamins. But no more steroids.

And I told Cooney.

"We never talked about your disobeying my instructions at the Santa Maria game," Cooney said after practice one day that week. We were in his cluttered office, with him in the master position, behind the desk. He played with a pencil, alternately tapping it on a finger or screwing the point into his palm.

"Yeah . . . well . . . it worked, didn't it? Isn't that what counts?" Ordinarily I'd have dropped down on the wooden swivel chair near his desk, but there was something about his attitude that didn't invite informality.

"Sit down," he barked, motioning to the chair. "If you'd have followed my directions, we'd have done even better!"

I bit back a disrespectful snort, dropped down on the hard seat, and crossed my legs.

"On my team, you do what you're told! You don't look the other way when I signal instructions!"

I shrugged. "They were mowing us down! If we'd followed your directions we'd have been killed!"

"Listen, Potter. Don't think you're so smart. I want you to know I saved your ass. I covered for you with those scouts, didn't let on what you were up to. If they'd

known, you'd be dead with them! Scholarship kaput!"
He ran a finger across his throat.

"I don't think so," I said, feeling my face grow hot.

"Oh you don't, do you?"

"No. I think they'll sign me whether or not I put on all that extra weight!" I crossed my fingers in my lap and stared right into Cooney's eyes.

"Meaning?"

"Meaning—I'll take my chances that I'm good enough just as I am."

Cooney laughed, without smiling. "Good-bye State. Good-bye all the other schools that thought you had potential."

I thought about Mike, which made it easier not to be intimidated, and didn't answer.

Cooney was back to tapping the pencil on his finger. He shrugged finally and said, "Well, if that's what you've decided, fine. It's your life. I wish you luck." He looked over his papers as if he'd lost all interest in me. "However. You know the rules. You disobeyed my orders. I'm going to have to put you on suspension."

I nodded, repressing a grin. He had to penalize me to save face. But the guys would know. And with the season over, it had no significance anyway.

"All right. Get out of here," he growled. "And I don't want to see you around for the next two weeks!"

I left his office with head bowed. No use in rubbing it in. Halfway across the gym I sprinted ahead, jumping in the air and letting out a subdued "Yeouw!"

Maybe I was an optimist, but I wanted to believe I'd gotten off steroids in time, that Mike would somehow make it, that Cooney would get his—and that at least one scholarship would come through.

And then I felt free to think about other things. Laurel, for instance. And Saturday.

Afterword

As many as half a million male American high school seniors have used or are using anabolic steroids, many of them in large doses over extended periods of time, according to a survey reported in the December 16, 1988 issue of the *Journal of the American Medical Association.*

Participants in this study were twelfth-grade males in forty-six private and public high schools across the country. Results indicate that 6.6 percent of them started using steroids at age sixteen and even younger. Most said they took the black-market drugs in hopes of improving their athletic performance. But more than a quarter of the users said their prime reason was to "look good; to pick up girls," according to Dr. Richard H. Strauss, a steroid expert. The study suggests that steroids have become drugs of abuse among teenagers and the side effects of steroids may be especially serious in adolescents.

Among the risks anabolic steroid users face, according to recent studies, are:

HEART DISEASE   In only six weeks the drugs cause a dramatic increase in cholesterol levels and a decrease in the protective HDL (high-density lipoprotein), bringing levels to that of severe coronary disease patients awaiting bypass surgery.

SEXUAL AND REPRODUCTIVE DISORDERS   Use results in atrophy of the testicles, loss of libido, impotence, and in women menstrual irregularity, deep voices, hairiness, and infertility.

IMMUNE DEFICIENCIES   White blood-cell production is suppressed so that the immune system is less able to fight off viruses and cancer.

LIVER DISORDERS   Serious liver damage, including jaundice and tumors, as well as gallstones result. Half the athletes who use steroids develop abnormal liver function tests.

STUNTED GROWTH   In teenagers who have not completed growth, the steroids can close the growth plates in the long bones and permanently stunt their growth.

PSYCHOLOGICAL DISTURBANCES   Increases hostile and aggressive behavior. Former wives of football players who used steroids said their husbands became super aggressive and sexually violent. Severe depression can follow discontinuance of steroid use.

Jim Hill, former safety for the San Diego Chargers and Green Bay Packers and Sports Director for KABC-TV in Los Angeles, speaking for most athletes, says, "It's stupid to use them [steroids] because they can kill. The long-term effects are physically harmful and can cause permanent damage."

About the Author

GLORIA D. MIKLOWITZ is the author of many books for teenagers, including *Did You Hear What Happened to Andrea?*, *The Love Bombers*, *Close to the Edge*, *The Day the Senior Class Got Married*, *The War Between the Classes*, *Love Story, Take Three*, *Secrets Not Meant to Be Kept*, and *Good-bye Tomorrow*. Her most recent book for Delacorte Press was *The Emerson High Vigilantes*.

Ms. Miklowitz teaches writing and lives in La Cañada, California, with her family.